The Fractured Mind.

Ottavio Lepore

Copyright page

This is a work of fiction. Names, characters, places and incidents either are the product of the author's imagination or are used fictitiously, and any resemblance to actual persons, living or dead, business establishments, events, or locales is entirely coincidental.

THE FRACTURED MIND

1

Acknowledgements

I have to start by thanking my friend Kaitlyn. From reading early drafts to giving advice on edits and to push me to keep going forward. This book wouldn't be complete without you.

Thank you to both my editors Ben Wolf and Pamela Cyran, you guys helped me a tremendous amount.

Thank you to Alyssa for creating the awesome cover and supporting me throughout the entire journey.

Thank you to all my friends and family for supporting me and helping me along this journey, it's been a hell of a ride.

I am eternally grateful for all of you.

Table of Contents

Chapter 1...4
Chapter 2...24
Chapter 3...34
Chapter 4...41
Chapter 5...58
Chapter 6...63
Chapter 7...70
Chapter 8...75
Chapter 9...83
Chapter 10...96
Chapter 11...123
Chapter 12...159
Chapter 13...168
Chapter 14...175
Chapter 15...181
Chapter 16...184
Chapter 17...211
Chapter 18...216
Chapter 19...219
Chapter 20...221
Chapter 21...225
Chapter 22...228
Chapter 23...235
Chapter 24...255
Chapter 25...272
Chapter 26...274
Chapter 27...276

CHAPTER 1

Ryan could hear the howling of the wind outside, he paused packing his luggage to listen. The cold winds of winter were slowly arriving, a sure sign that fall was nearing its end. Ryan soon returned to packing his things. He was planning a short trip out of town to a small rental house on the beach a few hours outside of Blackridge, the town in which he lived. Unfortunately, Ryan was not very good at packing—aside from over packing things he didn't need, he always forgot something he did. He decided to bring a large assortment of clothes, including shorts, jeans, shirts, and jackets. He stuffed them all inside his suitcase and prayed that it would close. After some struggling and removing a potentially excessive down jacket, he finally clasped the suitcase closed. Should he bring his laptop? His camera? He wasn't sure he would need them, much less use them, while on vacation. Nevertheless, he settled on bringing his camera and some accessories, hoping he would be able to get some scenic pictures.

While digging through his closet for some of the attachments, he found a long-lost book given to him by Hannah. He looked over the book, some of the pages were bent and the cover was somewhat ripped. He sighed, he felt bad he never finished it, it was one of her favorites. The book now sat in his closet neglected and forgotten. He imagined reading it with his toes in the sand by the ocean, so he added it to his bag. Again the feeling of him forgetting something overwhelmed him. He quickly had to push the feeling away, he didn't have much time before Hannah showed up to take him to his new vacation home by the beach. He did another once-over of his apartment to make sure everything was shut off and put away. Hannah had agreed to take care of his things while he was away, but he still wanted everything to be in order before he left.

Just as he finished his last round of the house, the doorbell rang. Assuming Hannah had arrived, Ryan grabbed his stuff, ready to head out. As he opened the door, he was surprised to see it was not Hannah but instead his neighbor, John.

"Oh, hey John. Is there something I can help you with?" inquired Ryan.

"Just wanted to let you know that the rent is due soon," responded John.

"Yeah, I already paid it, so you don't need to worry about me, thanks," said Ryan coldly. John was a very nosy neighbor. He was another tenant of the apartment building but somehow thought he owned the building. Ryan didn't mind it too much because he was barely ever home, but he still gave Ryan an uneasy feeling in his stomach.

"I see. Have a good trip," said John as he walked away.

"Thank you?" responded Ryan, confused. He never told anyone he was going on a trip. Strange, but Ryan was glad he wouldn't see his pesky neighbors for a while.

Ryan settled down in a chair by the dining table after he realized that Hannah had still not arrived.

I wonder what would be taking her this long? She's usually so punctual. Maybe there was traffic or something. He tried to reason why Hannah would be late without thinking the worst, *what if she was hurt?* Ryan tried to push the intrusive thoughts out but they weighed heavily on him. *This is all my fault, if it wasn't for me she wouldn't be hurt. Or even worse….* The doorbell rang, Ryan still felt tense, *what if there are police officers waiting to tell me Hannah's hurt or…dead?* Ryan opened the door with a shaky hand, but when he saw who was on the other side, a wave of relief washed over him.

"Took you long enough. I didn't realize that you had come from Pluto to pick me up," Ryan snarked.

"Well, I had to make a quick stop before I came here. Deal with it. I'm doing you a favor," responded Hannah with a subtle anger in her voice. Ryan shifted uncomfortably, it was strange to see her in a bad mood.

"And I am thankful for that, but I would like to get there on time," Ryan said with a smile, trying to read Hannah's mood.

"Just get your stuff and let's get a move on. It'll take us a while to get there," she responded flatly.

"Oh-kay…is everything alright? You seem a little mad," said Ryan lightly. He wanted to avoid angering her any more.

"I'm fine. Let's just go," responded Hannah, turning her back to him. Ryan grabbed his stuff and began to walk out of his apartment. Something was different. Ryan could feel a chill from talking to Hannah. It was as if he had done something to upset her. As much as it burned in his mind to ask her what was going on, he dropped the subject before he made it worse.

As Ryan loaded up the car, Hannah checked her phone to make sure all roadways were clear.

"It doesn't look like there's any traffic at all. We should have a smooth ride out there," explained Hannah.

"Well let's hope that doesn't change. Usually there's no traffic right before an accident hits," said Ryan. "Why do you always have to be so pessimistic?" said Hannah angrily. Now it was clear something was the matter.

"It's what I do. What's your problem?" asked Ryan, now also starting to feel anger rise within him.

After hearing him pick up an angry tone, Hannah stayed silent. Ryan proceeded to finish loading the car and had tried to calm himself down, but his mind was racing a thousand miles a minute. Ryan did not often get angry, especially at Hannah, but there was something off between the both of them. This was not how he had planned to leave for vacation: being angry with Hannah, leaving his work behind, and everything was just starting to pile up with bitterness. He only needed about a day or two to relax and then he would be ready to get back to work. Was that so much to ask for? Ryan pondered for minute before entering the car. Hannah did not immediately start it. Instead, she kept her hands on the wheel, visibly white from the tension of gripping the steering wheel.

"What's wrong?" asked Ryan again.

"Nothing," Hannah responded coldly.

Ryan took a deep breath and did not pursue the conversation any further. Sometimes leaving things alone is the best resolution.

Hannah reluctantly moved her hand to the keys and slowly turned the key to start the ignition. The car roared to life.

Hannah being so distant and on edge was very unlike her. But that's not to say it never happened. Often times, Ryan would dig a larger hole trying to get her to open up and speak her mind. Since they had known each other for nearly a decade, Ryan had learned by now that she just needed space.

Hannah moved her hand from the keys not to the shifter, but into her jacket pocket, from which she pulled a box. It was tall, rectangular, and covered in black leather with a golden latch on the front. The leather was very clean and smooth--it was polished very recently.

Hannah placed the box on her lap, running her fingers over the corners, starting at the back of the box and moving her fingers forward slowly to the latch.

"I care about you Ryan," she said softly, her voice breaking the tender silence.

Ryan was eager to know what was in the box, but the tension lingered in the air around them like a dense fog.

"This is what took so long," said Hannah.

"You stopped to buy a box?" Ryan questioned with eyebrows raised.

He could tell by the look he received from Hannah that it was not a laughing matter.

"Sorry, I'm just not in a good mood," responded Ryan, trying to cover up his attitude.

"Obviously," said Hannah. The only thing colder than her tone was her stare. "But I want you to have this so that even when you're ridiculously far from home, I will always be with you. Even if you can't see or hear me," she said while slowly opening the box. She paused with the box about halfway open.

There was a faint glimmer from the inside, sharp and bright. She looked over to Ryan before shutting the box and handing it over to him. The weight surprised him more than anything. For such a simple box, it was quite heavy. What could possibly be in it?

As Ryan moved his fingers around the box, he noticed that the leather was smooth but was in fact very old. It was very worn and greying in some areas, but it felt extremely soft under his fingers. It was clearly well taken care of, but there was something else that Ryan noticed that bothered him more. It looked very expensive. Ryan enjoyed many of the gifts given to him by Hannah, but he still hated receiving them, and this seemed costlier than any previous gift. It made Ryan tense.

Ryan stared at Hannah for minute and ran his fingers around the edges. He found a groove where the box separated and used his thumb on his right hand to slowly lift the box open. The box creaked open and inside the box were two dark, steely strands of wire in a tight coil. The two strings pointed downward and joined at the top link of a jewel. It was stunning.

The colors were blindingly powerful, deep and clear. It looked exactly like a sunset. At the top, it was an exceedingly pale orange and yellow combination that slowly transitioned downward to a deep, dark ruby red. There were streaks of yellow like lightning all going to a fixed point at the bottom. Ryan was so focused on the colors he had not realized that it was in the shape of a heart.

Ryan ran his fingers under the cold chain and lifted the heart out of the box. In the sunlight, the jewel shone brightly, leaving flecks of golden sunshine all over Ryan's face. Ryan had a hard time looking away. It reminded him of a beautiful sunset he witnessed on a hike a few weeks back. He remembered seeing how beautiful Hannah had looked on that mountain, with the sunset behind her. Ryan felt himself blush, he scratched his face to try and play it off.

"They call it a Witch Stone. They're pretty rare and not many are this clear," Hannah explained. "I found it in the little pawn shop on the outskirts of town. It was hidden away really well," Hannah said enthusiastically. "And it was cheap," she added quickly, knowing how Ryan felt about gifts. "Look, I know you don't really like jewelry, but I thought this was really pretty and it's a great memento. Plus, if you secretly hate it, you can sell it and make a good amount of money," Hannah added, chuckling to herself.

"I—I don't know what to say," Ryan said, choked up. Hannah was right, he did not like jewelry, but there was something about the stone that comforted Ryan. It reminded him of a simpler time. When he was younger, he used to lay in his parent's hammock all summer and watch the sun set each and every day. It was one habit that he absolutely loved.

He'd told Hannah many memories of those nights, watching the sun change colors from orange and yellow to purple and blue, like a fire that changed colors depending on the type of ink burned. Ryan would watch in awe every night to see which type of sunset it would be. Thinking back on those nights, Ryan could always find solace. He remembered being comforted with his own memories of being alone with no worry in the world, just him and the sun.

"It's absolutely wonderful. I love it. Thank you so much," said Ryan as he pulled Hannah in for a warm hug.

"I'm glad you like it. I was worried you might hate it. But, you know if you don't like it, I can always take it back," said Hannah sweetly, biting her lower lip.

Ryan twirled the stone over and over in his hand before he unhooked the clasp and wrapped it around his neck. It gleamed in the sunlight as it dangled against his chest. It was truly the best gift Ryan had ever gotten.

"I love it" said Ryan quietly.

Once Hannah was satisfied, they set off. The house Ryan was staying at was about two hours away with no traffic. They talked about anything that came to mind, from traveling, to memories, hopes, dreams and even regrets.

About one hour into the trip, Ryan decided to ask a question that would resolve a lot of doubts in his mind, but also one that pushed on some boundaries he wasn't sure Hannah would be willing to cross.

"So, can we talk about what happened the other night or—" Ryan left his question unfinished.

"There's nothing to talk about. What happened, happened. There's nothing more we need to discuss," said Hannah softly, tightening her grip on the wheel.

"What do you mean there's nothing to talk about? We broke up months ago and what happened the other night was no accident. That's not something that should be brought up?" said Ryan, anger rising in his chest.

"No. What happened the other night was a mistake. There's nothing I can do to take it back, but if I could, I would. I don't want to give you the wrong idea, we're not getting back together," responded Hannah coldly.

"I don't get a say in this?" He asked.

"I know your opinion, and I know you want to get back together, but I don't agree with it," said Hannah.

Ryan took a minute to process what he was hearing. "So I'm not worth anything to you, is that it?" Ryan said, almost in a whisper.

"You don't understand what it was like being with you. You're neurotic, obsessive, jealous, and you always have a negative opinion about everything. It was hell trying to do anything with you!" yelled Hannah. She paused before continuing now with tears in her eyes. "I'm sorry but we're not compatible in that way. We want different things, and I can't go through that again."

Ryan stared at her. He could not have imagined this as her response. Ryan felt a pain welling up inside of him. He was at a loss for words but continued to stare at her with his mouth slightly ajar.

"I'm sorry, but how long do you think we could really last? We fight all the time," Hannah said softly.

"We can try to make it work, all relationships need to be worked on." Said Ryan

"Ryan, I love you, I always will but I don't think I can put myself through that again, I can't handle your constant mood swings and your negativity and paranoia," said Hannah. Her words spit like venom.

"So why get me the gift? It doesn't seem like something a 'friend' would do," he spat in return.

"Because I care about you and I love you, I just don't think you're ready for a relationship." Hannah said softly, she sounded hurt.

Ryan said nothing in return. Instead, he looked out of the passenger side window, following the trees as they passed by like green smears in an oil painting.

Hannah tried grabbing his hand but it was swiftly brushed sway by Ryan, he turned to face her, and as he did, he felt sick, he wanted out of this car as soon as possible.

"Don't. Please, don't." Ryan was almost begging her. "I thank you for driving me but I think this conversation is—"

Before Ryan could finish his sentence, there was a sudden jolt.

The car moved in slow motion. He heard nothing but the crunch of bone against metal. Windows shattered and sent pieces of glass tearing through Ryan's skin. Hot blood streamed down his face. A sharp pain gripped his arm, and the seat belt cut into his skin.

The seatbelt applied fierce pressure over his chest, and Ryan could barely breathe. The car toppled over and his hair stood on end as if he were underwater, falling back to his scalp when the car was upright. His mind went blank, he felt nothing but the fear of fighting to stay alive as the car collapsed around him with every flip. After what seemed to be an eternity, the car finally settled.

Ryan's now swollen eyes could barely see anything, and the ringing in his ears was almost unbearable. Ryan tried to move out of his seat, but his body wouldn't respond to his commands. The car crumpled like an empty soda can with Ryan and Hannah stuck inside.

Ryan couldn't see Hannah's face. It was covered by her blood-matted hair, and she leaned onto the airbag, limp. Ryan didn't know if she was conscious.

Ryan's hearing slowly returned, with it came a soft *plip, plip, plip*. Ryan looked down to see droplets of blood forming at his nose. They dropped and exploded onto the airbag before continuing to roll down the side of the bag. Ryan could barely keep himself awake, his head was splitting, his entire body ached. He heard sirens in the background, amplifying his pain. His neck weakened. He placed his head on the now-deflating airbag and let his eyes close.

Ryan drifted in and out of consciousness. He faintly heard the mechanical whirring of power tools. The door broke away and cold air entered quickly. The blood on his face had dried, but a chill emanated from where the blood once flowed.

The cool air comforted Ryan and he took a breath. Excruciating. He gasped at the surge of pain in his chest with each breath, causing him even more pain, a vicious cycle.

The seatbelt was cut from under him, though he could not see whose hands were grabbing him. They were powerful and cold. Ryan's hand was stuck, and when he was being pulled out, Ryan let out a large yelp. Someone tried to free his hand but had no luck.

Ryan heard the whirring again but soon lost consciousness. Ryan could feel the breeze drift in from where the roof had been. Ryan lifted his head up as far as he could, the light burned his eyes. The frigid air stung in his throat. Ryan was dizzy. He could see white blurs falling towards him. They landed on his cheek, leaving a short, watery impression. It was snowing. The snowflakes drifted aimlessly through the air before settling on Ryan's warm skin. He watched them dance in front of his eyes, falling gently before landing and disappearing in tiny pools of blood all over Ryan's face.

He could feel himself being laid down. It was soft. He could feel straps being tied down around him and a stiff collar being put around his neck. The whirlwind of falling snow lulled him as he felt his consciousness drift away from him once more.

CHAPTER 2

Ryan stirred but didn't have the energy to move. He opened his eyes, but the bright sunlight burned. His eyelids flickered as he tried again, with slightly more success the second time around. The burning light brought tears to his eyes. He tried to lift his left arm, but nothing happened.

Fear welled in his stomach. He couldn't move his fingers, and his vision was too blurry to see anything. His ears still rang, but he could hear the slightest bit of varied tones in it now. It was a very faint voice but not one that he recognized.

Ryan sat back and waited until his vision cleared. As he began to make out some faint shapes nearby, he noticed that the room was exceptionally white. There was a TV monitor directly across from him airing a news program. Ryan could barely pay attention, all he was able to understand was there was a severe car crash on the highway with three injured and one dead. Ryan saw the mangled carnage of the scene, there was a lot of blood. Ryan vaguely recalled the reporter saying that one of the cars jumped the barricade and crashed into the other before the TV was switched off. Next to him was a man in a white coat resting his arm on a machine. The doctor was speaking to someone with his back towards Ryan. The other person placed the TV remote on one of the bedside tables.

Ryan tried to speak but nothing would come out. His throat was dry and felt like he had swallowed shards of glass. He needed water. As he tried to sit up the machines next to him began to beep more rapidly. The man noticed and turned around as if Ryan was rudely interrupting him.

"Hello, Mr. Stark. My name is Dr. Richard Ulric. You are in Saint Maria Hospital. Do you know why you're here?" said Dr. Ulric.

Ryan cleared his throat; it stung to swallow. He put all his effort into opening his mouth and trying to get his lungs to work properly.

"...no," Ryan said, barely audible

"That's not a surprise after the trauma you have been through," said Dr. Ulric softly. "You have been in a very severe car accident, Mr. Stark. You arrived at this hospital in critical condition. Your left arm was broken in seven places, we had to put in a series of pins and plates, but you will have proper use of the arm after physical therapy.

"Your right leg sustained severe muscular and nerve damage. The good news is that the femur is still intact. It'll be sore for a few weeks and it'll be difficult to walk, but your physical therapist will assist you in getting back on your feet in no time," said Dr. Ulric

Ryan's mind was buzzing. He couldn't think straight, and his heart hurt from beating so hard, it felt as if someone was squeezing his chest. Ryan bent his left arm at the elbow and tried to bring it eye level to see how it was. He couldn't see anything but bleached white bandages covering his arm and a few fingers. The fingers that were exposed were purple and swollen. They did not look like his fingers at all.

"You have been in and out of consciousness for several days now, so you had better take it easy," said Dr. Ulric as he picked up a clipboard with what seemed to be several pages of paper on it. He began to turn away from Ryan, scribbling something down.

Ryan grunted but nothing came out. He released a short breath and clutched his sides. The noise was enough to catch Dr. Ulric's attention. He turned to look back at Ryan.

Straining to get words out, Ryan tried as hard as he could still clutching his sides, "Hannah. What ha...ppened Hannah?" asked Ryan weakly.

"What's that?" asked Dr. Ulric.

Ryan stared at him for a while and took a quick short breath. He released it slowly while he spoke. "Ha...nnah," Ryan said, slightly louder.

"Oh, that's the driver of the vehicle?" responded Dr. Ulric toneless.

Ryan couldn't bear to talk anymore. He just nodded his head slowly.

"Well, a colleague of mine operated on her. Her injuries were far worse than the ones you sustained. It seems at the last moment she tried turning the car so the driver's side sustained most of the damage. She was stable when she was brought in, but her condition worsened, and she's currently in the intensive care unit. I can assure you she is being well taken care of, but it is unknown what the extent of her injuries are until she regains consciousness," said Dr. Ulric sternly. It seemed he did not want to discuss it any further. There was nothing Ryan could do in his condition anyway.

"Rest up, Mr. Stark. It'll be a long journey to recovery. We'll talk more in the morning," assured Dr. Ulric as he patted Ryan's shoulder, and Ryan winced at the pressure.

Dr. Ulric left the room, leaving only what Ryan had figured was a nurse behind. She walked over and was looking at the machines and writing down information. Ryan had no idea what she needed it for, but he didn't care. He looked back at his hand but slowly turned his gaze up to the ceiling. The blinding white room continued to make Ryan's eyes hurt.

He closed his eyes and felt them welling up behind his eyelids. Soon he felt the tears slip out and start to trail down his cheeks. Ryan tried his best to keep quiet and cry softly but was slowly losing the battle. He turned away from the nurse, he didn't like when people saw him cry. He saw what was left of his belongings in a clear plastic bin off to his right side. He assumed there weren't many things left from the crash.

From this distance Ryan could see a black box with the leather ripped from the sides. Underneath the leather-bound box was a white shell, stained pink from what Ryan could only assume was blood. He also saw parts of his wallet and watch, but couldn't see anything else.

In that moment, Ryan grabbed for the necklace that used to hang around his neck, but there was nothing there. The nurse had been watching him and took a deep breath. She went over to the plastic bin and opened the ripped box. From the inside she used both hands to scoop the necklace out and placed the remaining pieces on Ryan's bed sheets. When Ryan saw it, he gasped and let out short sobs.

The necklace was nearly broken beyond recognition. The only piece that was left intact was a shard of jewel that was about an inch in length. There weren't even enough pieces left to put it back together. Ryan continued to weep as the nurse spoke. She had a thick southern accent.

"Y'know, there were more pieces," she paused as if unsure she should go on. "They were embedded in your chest, and they had to be surgically removed," she continued in the softest voice she could use.

"I know how hard this can be. My name is Sally, and I'll be your nurse, so if you need anything don't be afraid to give me a holler, sweetie," Sally added after a minute of uncomfortable silence.

Ryan turned to face her. She was an attractive woman in her late forties, with golden blonde hair and bright blue eyes. Her cheeks had creases where years of smiling had left their mark. She had a very gentle face and was very kind so far. Ryan placed his head back on his pillow and wiped the tears away with his good hand.

"Thank you," said Ryan dryly.

"Not a problem, honey. So is there any family we can contact? someone you want to know that you're here?" she said sweetly.

Ryan's mind immediately went to Hannah, she was the only one that would care.

"No thank you, my mom passed away a few years ago and I haven't spoken to my father in years," he said softly. The death of his mother still pained him, he could feel his throat go dry, a sure indication that he would start crying again.

"Alright well if you think of anyone or need me I'll be in the hall, just push this button here." Sally pointed to a button in the shape of a small person on the side of Ryan's bed before quickly making her exit.

Ryan made a fist and tears began streaming down his face. Everything hurt. It hurt to exist. Hannah was the only thing stable in his life. He couldn't begin to imagine a life without her. He closed his eyes tightly to stop the burning and the tears. Soon, he fell swiftly into a deep sleep once more.

CHAPTER 3

Ryan awoke sometime later but something was different. The room was extremely dark, and it was a strange red hue. It was strange to see everything so dark in a hospital. Ryan looked down and he was in his regular clothes on a torn and stained mattress. He swung his legs off the bed and noticed he no longer had any pain. No bandages or casts, and it felt great. This didn't make sense.

Ryan smiled widely. He felt as good as new. He got up and walked to the door.

"Hello?" Ryan called as he peered around the door frame. His voice seemed to echo down the hall. It was eerily quiet. Ryan walked out of the room and down the hallway. It was completely empty: no chairs, no gurneys, and no other doors. It was just a straight path that he couldn't see the end of.

Ryan continued walking for a while, just watching the wall. Every now and then, there would be a hole in the wall exposing electrical wires and rusted rebar. Ryan could swear when he passed these holes he could hear a wailing woman, he could faintly hear her say "There's no one here" but he wasn't brave enough to move closer.

Ryan began sweating. The hall felt never ending until he saw a change ahead: a rusted set of doors. Finally, Ryan had reached an elevator. He clicked the button to take the elevator down but nothing happened, he pushed the button several more times but still nothing. He wasn't sure where to go, but there was a door off to the right that he assumed would lead to the stairs. Ryan turned to face it. It used to be white, but it was heavily stained with an unknown substance. There were dark splotches close to the bottom of the door as if something had seeped through. It was strange to see in a hospital.

Ryan grasped the handle and it started to crumble in his hand. He only had one chance to open it. He spun the handle quickly and pushed on the door. The door swung open.

Ryan opened his hand to free the remaining bits of handle and watch them crumble to the floor. He picked the largest piece he could find and slid it underneath the door to act as a doorstop. He began to walk into the room, his right fingertips skimming the wall next to him. His fingers reached a light switch, and he give it a gentle nudge up. The lights flickered before finally giving a consistent glow.

The light was one single bulb hanging, and it gave the room a yellow hue. It was dark and musty even with the light on. There was a certain stench in the room that made Ryan's eyes water. His eyes were drawn to a black bag lying atop a bloodied gurney.

A body bag, and it looked full. Ryan's heart leapt into his throat, the hairs on the back of his neck stood straight up, and the blood in his hands ran ice cold.

Should I open it? It doesn't make sense for there to be only one body bag in an entire hospital. Is that me? Am I a dead?

Ryan's head started hurting, he ignored it the best he could. Ryan walked very slowly towards it. It felt as though it took at least 10 minutes to reach the gurney. Ryan raised his hand to the zipper only to realize that he was shaking violently. He took a deep breath and held it in. He could feel his heartbeat in his ears.

He grabbed the zipper, which felt cold even to Ryan's icy fingers. The cold seemed to burn him, but he began to unzip the bag anyway. The zipper was slowly descending the length of the bag, the sound ringing in his ears. His vision blurred. He gulped and began to take short, labored breaths. His legs began to lose feeling and go wobbly underneath him. He pried the bag open and looked inside, but what he found made him nearly collapse. He grabbed the edge of the gurney and tried desperately to hold himself up.

He looked inside the bag and saw himself, pale white with deep purple scars all over his body. His mind went numb.

Is this my real body?

Ryan reached one hand up and kept the other on the gurney to keep himself steady. Ryan's fingers were shaking as he reached to touch the body's cheek when his eyes—the body's eyes—opened. They were glazed over and completely white, with no discernible iris. Ryan screamed and fell backwards.

The body on the table began to rise from the waist up and stared directly at him. Ryan tried to get up as quick as he could but could feel his legs failing him. He was sliding along the floor trying to get as much distance as possible between himself and the zombie version of himself.

When Ryan finally found his footing, he got up and ran out of the door. The elevator button was now glowing, Ryan quickly tapped the button to call the elevator, and before long, it had reached his floor. He turned to see if his body was chasing him but there was nothing. The elevator doors opened, and just as Ryan turned to face the elevator the blinding lights of a car barreling towards him appeared.

Ryan screamed at the top of his lungs and covered his face.

Ryan sat up startled and in a cold sweat. The EKG machine next to him was beeping violently. The pain was excruciating. It burned his whole body. He was being held down by hands that he assumed belonged to Dr. Ulric and Sally. Ryan could feel his heartbeat throb underneath the cast on his arm.

His heart hurt and he couldn't grasp what he just saw. Ryan was breathing very heavy and each breath hurt in his chest. Ryan could feel the doctor pushing his icy hands down on his shoulder and bicep. It was soothing as he noticed he was sweating.

He turned his gaze on the nurse, who held a large syringe in her hand. She pressed the needle into a vial and slowly withdrew the plunger until a clear liquid filled the syringe. She was quick to transfer the needle straight into Ryan's arm. This caused Ryan to panic more as he tried to pull his arm away he noticed Dr. Ulric was still holding him firmly in place.

"Ryan! You need to sit still, you ripped your IV out!" hissed Dr. Ulric. "It's only a sedative! Relax!"

Ryan could feel his strength fading. His eyes felt heavy and his breathing had slowed tremendously. He could hear them talk but the words were garbled and sounded like white noise. His vision was fading to black and, before Ryan could move, he had fallen asleep

CHAPTER 4

Ryan opened his eyes to the sound of birds whistling. The sounds hurt his head. He wanted the noises to stop, to just sit in complete silence and pray his headache would go away. His arm was sore and burned. Ryan looked down and saw his elbow was completely covered in bandages. They needed to be changed as they were stained a dark red.

"Mr. Stark, you gave us quite a scare last night," stated Dr. Ulric in a firm tone. Ryan was startled to see the doctor standing next to him, he hadn't even noticed.

"You had a nightmare and were thrashing rather violently. You ripped out your IV."

Ryan turned to look at his arm; the red of the bandages surprised him, had he really lost that much blood? The bandages were now saturated to a deep ruby red. It was at this moment that Sally came over and began to change the bandages.

Ryan cleared his throat. "I didn't realize. I'm sorry."

He was shocked that he was coherent, his throat had nearly completely healed, and he finally heard his voice for the first time since the accident. This realization caused Ryan to think, *how long has it been since the accident*

"It's quite alright. I can imagine after the ordeal you've been through that you would have nightmares," said Dr. Ulric coolly.

Ryan actually had no issue with the accident. He was more worried about Hannah since he hadn't heard anything about her condition. Ryan turned to the doctor.

"How long has it been?" he said, swallowing loudly.

"It's been about nine days," said Dr. Ulric, flexing his jaw.

Ryan groaned and looked back at the middle of the room. He could see his reflection in the black glass of the TV. Ryan's face was distorted among the glass, but he knew he looked different even though he felt no swelling or pain in his face. It was strange.

After Sally had removed the old bandages, she grabbed some new gauze and Ryan raised a hand to stop her,

"I plan to take a shower. You can leave it off for now," said Ryan dryly.

She looked at Dr. Ulric and he nodded. She then left the room for a minute and returned with a plastic yellow tray.

"Hope you're hungry," Sally said as she placed the tray in front of Ryan. She pulled the top off and it revealed some dull yellow eggs with a side of bacon, a glass of orange juice, and a small container of a gelatin substance. Ryan pushed the gelatin container to the farthest corner of the tray.

"I'll let you enjoy your meal," said Dr. Ulric with a smirk.

"I'll try," said Ryan sarcastically.

"Sally here will be happy to help you with anything you may need. I would recommend, after your shower, to get out of the room for some fresh air. It's a beautiful day out," said Dr. Ulric. He turned and left the room swiftly.

"Would you like me to help you with that?" said Sally sweetly.

"That's alright, I think it'd be good for me to get myself moving a bit," he said with a quick smile.

"I know you're going through a tough time, sugar. If you need anything at all, please let me know," said Sally.

Sally reminded Ryan of his own mother, sweet and always trying to help in any way she could, since his father would seldom even remember they existed. Ryan felt sad, maybe after this whole ordeal was over, he would book a trip to visit her. Ryan had a feeling that his father did not visit her grave very often.

Ryan took a forkful of eggs and almost coughed it back up. They didn't taste like eggs and were dripping in a strange salty liquid. Ryan forced himself to swallow a forkful but did not return to them. Instead, he only ate the bacon, which was very chewy, Ryan's jaw ached before he was able to force it down. Ryan didn't expect much for hospital food but still, the food was depressing. Ryan slid the tray away from him and turned to face the nurse.

"Hey, uh, Sally, do you know anything about a woman who was with me?" asked Ryan. "We were in the car together when we crashed."

Her smile quickly faded into a frown.

"I don't know much about it. I heard y'all come in together, but I was assigned only to you," said Sally quietly, avoiding making eye contact with him.

Ryan turned his eyes away as he felt tears slowly creep towards his eyes. He felt so powerless. He just wanted to find Hannah and hear her sweet voice telling him that everything would be alright.

"I can try and find her for you," whispered Sally.

Ryan didn't say anything. He just nodded as he brushed his tears away with his right hand.

Sally left the room and when she returned she brought with her an electric wheelchair, which surprised Ryan, but it soon dawned on him that he could not urge the wheelchair forward with only one good arm.

Sally unhinged the metal side of the bedding and dropped it down.

"Whenever you're ready to go, just hop on in. If you need any help, don't hesitate to ask," she said quietly.

"I think I'd like a shower. Could you help me there?" whispered Ryan

Sally agreed with a smile. She moved her body under Ryan's right arm, and dug her left hand into Ryan's side. Ryan bit his lip to keep himself from yelling out. It was sore and bruised and it burned with every second of her touch.

Ryan lurched forward onto one leg. He shook under his own weight, and began to fall, but Sally held him firmly in place.

Sally didn't seem like it, but she was very strong. She held Ryan firmly in her grasp and lifted him back onto his foot. Ryan hopped on one foot towards the bathroom.

Once inside, Ryan felt Sally untie the knot holding his gown up. The cloth fell from his body and it revealed everything. Ryan felt no shame. After all, it was Sally's job. He was sure she had seen worse, but then again, Ryan didn't know what he looked like anymore.

Ryan hopped forward over the cloth and stopped in front of the mirror. Ryan took a large breath and released it. He turned to face the mirror and was shocked by himself. His chest was covered in small scars. They were small holes, as if he were pierced with shrapnel. He turned to see his left side and saw a flash of colors: purples, yellows, and greens. It horrified Ryan. He couldn't tell what his normal skin color was and what was bruised. After moving down his side he realized his ribs were beginning to stick out. Ryan hadn't realized how much weight he'd lost.

Ryan turned his gaze to his own face. His cheek was swollen, and his eyes were a dark pink. He assumed he was recovering from black eyes. Ryan saw his reflection but couldn't recognize who was staring back at him. It wasn't possible that the person standing before the mirror looked like that. It was nothing similar to what Ryan knew of himself.

Ryan felt a dark cloak of emotion drape over him. He felt angry and sad but also defeated. If he fell at this moment, he might never get up again. Ryan felt tears begin to stream down his cheeks and sniffled before moving towards the shower.

After he was showered and dressed in a new white gown, he fell into the wheelchair. His arm grazed a small apparatus that stood straight up from the arm of the wheelchair. It reminded him of an old Atari joystick.

"It's an electric wheelchair. That's the control. The power switch is right below that and the brake is next to your right side wheel," said Sally.

Ryan said nothing and stared at the black control rod.

Normally, this would be humiliating for him. He hated being cared for by other people, but this time he felt different. There was an emptiness inside him. Every noise echoed inside him like a drum. He felt numb. Cold and numb. Nothing made sense and Ryan had lost interest in everything. He needed to find Hannah.

Ryan felt the wheelchair shake as Sally began to push him around. She took him to what he assumed to be Hannah's room. She stopped right in front of a very large door. It was larger than the others and larger than his own. Next to the door was the number 563, and alongside it was a symbol, it was a white colored half-moon shape.

"Thanks Sally, I got it from here," said Ryan, sinking down into the chair.

"I'm not sure that's such a great idea, you being alone and all," said Sally, hesitating. She was still holding onto the wheelchair handles.

"Look, it's a big hospital. I'm sure if I need help, I can find it," spat Ryan.

She remained silent before releasing her grip on the chair and walking away from Ryan. With his good hand, Ryan forcibly opened the door and used the control to move the wheelchair into the doorway. He strained to pull himself in, but managed to finally get inside. Strangely enough, the door lead to another room.

The door in front of him this time was locked by keypad. The door looked heavy and Ryan was sure he wouldn't get in. He looked around and found Dr. Ulric peering through a large window into the room and scribbling on his clipboard.

"Dr. Ulric?" asked Ryan.

"Hello, Ryan. Glad to see you up and about," responded Dr. Ulric without looking up from his writing.

Ryan wheeled himself slowly over to him. Ryan sat as straight as he could until his eyes could just barely make it over the edge of the window. What he saw made his heart stop.

On the other side of the glass was a large bed surrounded by large machines with several different lights and sounds. It was almost cluttered. All the machines had tubes and wires coming from their core towards the large bed.

Inside the bed Hannah lay still.

Ryan fought to hold back tears, but it was too much to handle. It destroyed him and broke down what little he had left. It was awful, and he had to look away. Ryan could feel Dr. Ulric's eyes on him, they burned into the side of his head, Ryan raised his hand to his eyes to block Dr. Ulric`s view of him. The silence between the two men seemed to last forever. Dr. Ulric cleared his throat and began speaking again, but he sounded muffled and distant. Ryan had to focus to understand.

"She sustained extreme trauma to her head, chest, and legs. Her femur broke in two places and pierced an artery, and she's suffering from hemorrhaging in her thighs and skull. She has a collapsed lung, and we've had to operate on her left arm and her spine. She has around thirty rods to keep her bones in place. She's been in a coma since she got in. It's a miracle she's alive at all. I must tell you that even if she gets through this, she'll never be the same. She is most likely paralyzed from the neck down and will not be able to speak without the help of-" he was quickly cut off.

"How could you let this happen?" howled Ryan, "You were supposed to help her! How could you torment her like this?"

Ryan yelled, his voice growing louder and louder. His face felt hot and tears flowed down it. Hs throat was growing hoarse from the yelling.

"I am not a miracle worker, Mr. Stark," retorted Dr. Ulric, looking back over her. "She came to this hospital broken like a plate. I cannot prevent what happened. I must deal with things as they are. There was no better option. I can't put her back together, I can only move the pieces. The rest is up to her."

Ryan was at a loss for words. He could barely think straight, and the pain in his body disappeared. His heart was pumping loudly in his ears and his adrenaline was forcing his eyesight to blur with each thump of his heart.

"If it's any consolation, that could've been you in there," said Dr. Ulric.

"What?" said Ryan sharply, rage continuing to fill his mind

"When the accident occurred, Ms. Fiore turned her car so the impact was almost all focused on the driver's side of the vehicle. She took the blunt force of it all," said Dr. Ulric.

He moved away from the window and slowly made his exit. Ryan lost his bearings, and his voice was now gone. As his rage faded, he felt only sadness. He looked over at Hannah and felt empty. He was totally and utterly alone. This was all his fault.

Ryan returned to his room and was assisted back into his bed. His mind was racing but empty all at the same time. Time seemed to move in fast forward. It was around dinner time when Sally arrived with a meal for Ryan.

"You alright honey?" asked Sally in her calming southern accent.

Ryan remained quiet, he did not even turn to face her. He heard her sigh and place the dinner on the table in front of him and leave the room. Ryan grabbed the apple juice cup and took a sip. it was watered down and very tart but Ryan finished the juice and placed the cup down. He stared out the window and he watched the moon rise out of the black sea of night.

Ryan felt empty, a shell of a person. While he didn't express it well, Ryan cared very much for Hannah. Seeing her like that cut him down like a razor. He felt divided, like a miniature version of himself, drowning in a sea of despair. Hannah was the only person who had cared for Ryan besides his family. She was his closest friend in the world and the love of his life. Without her, Ryan was completely alone. He could not forgive himself for doing this to Hannah.

She didn't deserve this. She deserved better. A future, a husband—one that cared for her thousands of ways more than Ryan could—and kids. Their last conversation haunted Ryan. If he hadn't said anything, Hannah would have been fine.

Ryan's thoughts got the better of him and he felt himself slipping deeper into madness. He was driving himself insane with the constant bickering of his thoughts, and from that darkness, came a larger looming thought. The ultimate, terrible thought, as if someone spoke in his ear. It chilled him to the bone.

Why don't you just end it all and kill yourself?

Ryan could feel the mysterious feeling almost breathing on his neck. The frozen words came out and stung his skin.

It's all your fault. You would be better off just finishing it off, the voice whispered.

Ryan swallowed and felt a cold sweat creep over him. Should he do it? Would he even be able to? He closed his eyes felt himself slip into a deep sleep.

CHAPTER 5

Ryan woke in the hospital room again. Was this another nightmare?

Ryan kicked his legs off the edge of the bed, this time with more vigor. The floor was freezing, and in Ryan's jean pocket was the pendant given to him by Hannah—unbroken and in pristine condition. Strange.

Ryan began wandering down the hall of the hospital floor, only this time the hospital looked normal. The walls were pearly white, and the floor was clean and shiny. Ryan could smell a hint of perfume. It smelled like Hannah. A light scent of vanilla and currant. Ryan continued to follow the aroma and found Hannah's room once more, but the room was completely different.

There was no locking mechanism and Hannah was just there, in the middle of the room. There were no more machines, no tubes, nothing. Ryan's breath quivered, and he saw his breath come out in a misty cloud. Ryan shuddered from the cold. The door to her room was slightly ajar. He pushed on it, and it swung open swiftly without a sound. Ryan walked slowly towards Hannah's bed. His hand gently caressed the sheets covering her. They felt like sheets of ice. He looked down upon her.

She was pale as snow, her lips were ruby red, and her eyes were closed. It reminded him of the tale of Snow White, and Ryan had a sudden desire to kiss her. His hand began twitching as he reached up to touch her face. His fingertips felt the outline of her jaw, and as Ryan's hand touched Hannah, her eyes sprung open. They were opaque, completely white and iris-less. Hannah sat upright, and Ryan stumbled back. It all felt very familiar. He fell toward the ground and his heart was beating out of his chest.

Hannah stared at him as she swung her legs off the bed. Ryan stood up and began to run out of the room. The hospital changed now: the walls were deep red and covered in rust. Ryan cut his feet on the broken floor as he ran. He shot a gaze over his shoulder and Hannah was right behind him, her hospital gown ripped and bloodied near her abdomen. Her pale legs poked through the bottom of the grown and they were twisted and contorted. They looked as if they were backwards. They were covered in dried blood.

Ryan turned around and began running down the hall.

"You did this to me! You killed me," said a ghostly voice.

Ryan's heart was burning from beating so viciously.

"How could you do this to me? I trusted you!" shouted the voice. "Why…WHY?" screamed the shrill voice.

Ryan was breathing very heavily, and his chest burned, but he could not stop. He continued running until he reached a point where there was a gaping hole in the floor. Ryan could try to jump across, but it was risky. He couldn't think straight, and his heart was hurting him. Ryan felt a hand on his shoulder, and he turned quickly and stared directly into her face. Her eyes were streaming blood as if the entity was crying.

"Why?" repeated the voice.

Hannah reached up and touched his face with her hand. It felt as though she was stealing Ryan's soul. Everything went cold, and he felt weak. He stepped back to escape her grasp only to find himself falling into the pit. The hole he entered became minuscule. All the light was gone, and then Ryan opened his eyes.

Ryan snapped awake back in the hospital bed soaked in sweat. His gown clung heavily to his chest and arms. His arm was throbbing again. Ryan assumed it was very late into the night. He stirred and reached for the water near his bedside. He reached an arm out to grasp the cup, but he was shaking so much he could barely close his hand around it.

Ryan gave up trying to take a drink. Instead, he wiped the sweat off his face and tried to sit up as best he could, but the hospital bed was too soft for him to push himself up with his only good arm. Ryan realized he was breathing heavy. He tried to take deep breaths and slow his heart down.

Ryan's nightmares were getting worse each day he was in the hospital. He was barely sleeping. They were getting more and more detailed each day, and each one slowly tested the limits of Ryan's mind. He wished that once he left the hospital they would end, but something inside him said otherwise. Ryan could see the sun starting to rise behind the shades, but he wanted to try another hand at sleeping before fully waking for the day.

CHAPTER 6

Ryan stirred awake, but it was not to the sound of birds chirping or the gentle beep of the machines next to him. Instead, he was woken by loud shouting and a group of nurses running.

Nurses running? That's not good.

Ryan's heart sunk a little lower, and he feared the worst. What if they were running toward Hannah? He had to find out what was happening. He reached over the side of his bed and unhinged the metal barrier keeping him locked into the bed. It crashed to the side of the bed with a loud bang. No one seemed to notice. He removed the sheets covering his legs and lifted his heavily bandaged left leg up and over the edge. He pushed himself off the bed with his right leg, and it burned as he extended himself forward.

Ryan hopped as quickly as he could towards his wheelchair. He collapsed into it with a thud and quickly lowered the foot placements. He pushed the button on and a soft whirring began, indicating the chair had power. He pushed forward on the control rod and the chair lurched forward. It took Ryan a few seconds to get used to the controls, but he was soon out of his room and speeding down the hall. He went on for what seemed hours. He didn't remember how to get to Hannah's room.

"Excuse me, miss," said Ryan with one hand waving in the air.

A nurse in pink scrubs stopped beside him. He barely looked at her face. His mind was racing, and he had to get to Hannah fast.

"How can I help you, sir?" said the nurse

"I'm looking for a room, but I don't remember the number. I know there was a half-moon looking thing close to it. I don't know if that helps," stated Ryan desperate to find the room.

"It's down the hall. Make a right and then a left, and straight down. It'll be the last door on your right," replied the nurse.

"Thanks," said Ryan, and he moved his chair as fast as he could.

Ryan followed the instructions to the letter and soon arrived in front of the infamous large door. The half-moon symbol was staring back at him. Ryan entered the room, but this time, there was no one inside. He moved towards the window and a wave of relief flooded over him. Hannah was still laying idly, with no apparent change. Amongst his relief, another wave of sadness rushed over him. It pained him to see Hannah like this, and it stung Ryan to his core.

"I can let you into the room if you want."

Ryan was startled by the voice. He hadn't heard anyone come in. He turned to face the voice and found Dr.

Ulric. Ryan just stared at the doctor for a long time, but the doctor seemed unfazed by his glare. He just stood with his arms behind his back, waiting for Ryan's answer.

Ryan looked back and nodded slowly. The doctor moved swiftly to the keypad and entered a notably long number. The pad let out a long beep after accepting the code, and Dr. Ulric swung the door open. Ryan moved his wheelchair towards the door, the doctor glaring down at him.

"Thank you," said Ryan as he entered the room.

"You'll have about ten minutes with her," replied the doctor.

He shut the door behind him, and Ryan heard the lock click back into place. Ryan stared at Hannah. It was dead quiet in the room with the exception of the beeping of the heart rate monitor and the gentle swoosh of the lung machine. Ryan sat there for a minute before moving himself closer to her. When he was right beside her, Ryan began crying loudly. She looked to be in so much pain, and yet her face was emotionless.

Hannah's eyes had dark bruises surrounding them, and her lips were swollen and cracked from the lack of saliva or water. There was a patch of hair missing from her scalp, replaced with several dark stitches. He looked down her body and only her arms were exposed. The rest of her damaged body was hidden away from view.

Ryan placed his hand on hers and was disturbed to find it lukewarm. She was barely warm enough to keep herself alive. His tears blurred his vision. He firmly grasped her hand and slowly lowered his head close to hers.

He whispered in her ear as gently as he could. "I'm so sorry. I did this to you, it's all my fault," Ryan said through his sobs. "I never should have done this to you, and I hope you can recover. Please get better. I love you, Hannah. Please, keep fighting this."

The silence was broken abruptly, not by a person, but more by a sound. A sound that would haunt Ryan for days to come. Ryan stared at the machine opposite of him. The gentle beep, beep, beep of the heart monitor had been replaced with a haunting steady tone: the sound of Hannah flat lining filled his ears.

Ryan gasped in horror at the sight, "No, no, no, no! NO!" howled Ryan. He tried standing but failed and the wheelchair rolled away from him. Ryan felt the pain rise in his legs. He collapsed and grabbed the railing beside Hannah to support himself. Ryan's vision went blurry. His head was spinning.

He cried out, "Please don't do this Hannah!" Ryan spat. He was trembling.

He didn't hear the door open and the flood of doctors enter. It was a blur of white coats with another small wave of colored scrubs. Ryan did not even notice their faces. They spoke but there was no sound, everything was muted. Ryan grabbed Hannah's hand and could feel the warmth fading away from her. He watched his tears drop onto her hand with a soft *pop*. They exploded and left an oblong shape. Ryan felt several hands grab and restrain him as he tried to resist.

"No! I need to stay here! Hannah!" yelled Ryan. He pushed and used his hands to leverage himself off the powerful doctor, but it was useless. Ryan began sobbing and struggled to move at all. His strength left him, and Hannah left him. His love left him. He felt hollow.

CHAPTER 7

Ryan awoke in the familiar white room in the familiar bed. Like déjà vu, he stirred and found Dr. Ulric.

What hell is this?

Everything was exactly like when he first arrived at the hospital. He groaned at the familiar scenes. He was sick of staying in this hospital, and he just wanted to be done with it all. Nothing mattered anymore. He found himself crying once more.

Dr. Ulric looked up from his ever-present clipboard, puzzled, as if he didn't understand what Ryan was feeling. He pulled up a chair and sat down next to Ryan. He placed the clipboard on the machine next to him and slouched into the chair.

Ryan watched him the entire time and only met his eyes when he finally slouched down. He had just noticed they were bright blue. The doctor raised both hands up to his face and placed the index fingers of each hand into a triangle in front of his lips. He stared at Ryan for a long time before he spoke.

"How are you feeling?" asked the doctor.

"Is that a joke?" Ryan said coldly, squinting hard.

"I want to know," the doctor said monotonously.

"I feel like the embodiment of death. Everything is falling apart around me, and you expect me to talk about my feelings?" Ryan said slowly.

"But what are you feeling? What's inside your head or your chest? How are you dealing with all of this?" said the doctor, moving his hand around the room.

"It all sucks. I feel heartbroken and infuriated with you," Ryan retorted.

"Me? I haven't done anything to you," said the doctor, looking puzzled.

"You're condescending and you're just rubbing salt into my wounds," said Ryan raising his voice slightly.

"I am doing no such thing. I just want to know. What is going on in your mind?" said the doctor sternly.

Ryan was confused. He'd never been so pressed to explain his feelings.

The doctor just sat there waiting until Ryan spoke. He was very stubborn and tough.

"I feel bitter. I feel guilty. This is all my fault and I can't do anything about it. Hannah's dead, and it's because of me. I can't live with that," said Ryan, wiping tears from his face.

The doctor sat back into the chair and waited before speaking.

"Well, yes, she has passed. I think, however, it is foolish to blame yourself for it. It had nothing to do with you. She made a choice. She did what she had to do so you can continue to live. You can't soil her memory by laying down and dying," said the doctor softly.

The doctor stood up and pushed the chair back. His clipboard clattered to the floor. Ryan turned to look at it and realized the handwriting on it was very beautiful and formal. Ryan looked at it, perplexed, but turned away before the doctor noticed. Dr. Ulric bent down and picked the board up, glancing at Ryan before heading towards the door. The doctor stood in the doorway for a second before turning and speaking once more.

"They say that the candle that burns the brightest, burns half as long. I'm sorry for your loss. She was, as I believe, a wonderful woman." He tapped the door frame with the palm of his hand and walked out of the room.

Ryan continued to stare at the empty doorway. Then he turned his gaze up toward the ceiling, Dr. Ulric was right. He couldn't waste a life that was graciously given to him by Hannah's sacrifice. Ryan could feel his tears run down his cheeks toward his ears. He took a deep, shaky breath and let it out slowly. He sniffled at the air and his

tranquility was broken by Sally coming into the room.

"You should eat something," she said as she placed

another gray tray in front of Ryan.

Ryan sighed at the unveiling of the food. Nothing but gray

oatmeal with more apple juice and water, accompanied, of

course, by a small container of a gelatin dessert. Today it

was a neon blue, and it was at this moment that Ryan

decided he had to leave the hospital as soon as he could.

CHAPTER 8

Another week passed before Ryan was finally able to check out on his own. After a week of physical therapy his leg was still very sore, but with the use of crutches it was bearable.

He'd never had to sign so many forms in his life. The scribbles of his signature began to turn foreign to him, and halfway through, he had to stop to regain his memory of it. Ryan was rolled out of the hospital in a wheelchair. The skies were gray and the air was terribly cold. It was early winter now, and it smelled as if another snowfall was fast approaching.

Ryan sniffed at the air and could smell the familiar aroma of dry leaves and the cold. Hannah would love this weather. Winter was one of her favorite seasons. Often times, Ryan had caught Hannah staying up all night just to watch the first snowfall. She said that there was a peaceful serenity when the snow fell. Slow and steady the flakes would drift toward the ground, landing and layering until they were woven into thin blankets.

Hannah hated being in the snow but loved watching it. Something about its pure essence made her love seeing it.

I can't believe it. She's really gone.

His eyes began to burn and tear again. He tried to fight the tears from rolling and held his eyes shut tight. He didn't want to believe it. It just couldn't be real. As he opened his eyes, he saw the cab draw near. He wiped his tears with the back of his hand and sniffed hard to clear his nose. The cab pulled up, and Ryan hesitated. It was strange to go home without Hannah.

Ryan reached out and opened the cab door.

"You need any help?" said the driver with a thick Russian accent.

"No, I'm alright," Ryan said before he limped inside.

It was still difficult for him to perform everyday tasks with his leg. He directed the driver to his house and paid him. Ryan then realized he never checked his pockets after putting his clothes back on. He reached into his pockets and pulled out his now shattered phone and torn leather wallet. It made him chuckle. Nothing seemed to be strong enough to take it down. The wallet was a gift from his father nearly fifteen years ago. Aside from the slight fraying of the lining, the wallet was nearly perfect. Until now. Ryan touched his chest to find the necklace from Hannah. It was only then that he remembered it was gone, but he could feel his scars through his shirt. Tears started welling up in Ryan's eyes again when the car came to a dead stop.

"You here," rasped the driver. He clearly freshly immigrated from some country Ryan knew nothing about.

"Thanks," sniffed Ryan as he limped out of the cab. He gave the driver the fare and a tip in crumpled, slightly torn dollar bills. Some of them were stained with blood but the driver took them with gratitude, and the cab soon departed. Ryan turned to face his apartment building—he realized he had to go up several flights of stairs.

You can do this, he encouraged himself with great doubt weighing in his mind.

Ryan searched his pockets before reaching into his jacket to pull his apartment key out. As he was putting the key into the lock, he realized he was shaking. Ryan took a short breath and forced himself to keep steady. He slid the key into the lock and slowly turned it, waiting until the clicking of the lock had stopped. He pushed the door, but it didn't move. He pushed slightly harder and still the door stood still. Without much thought, Ryan pushed again, but this time with his shoulder. The pain he felt in his arm and chest was colossal. It knocked the breath from him.

The door swung open, and Ryan met his floor. He was gasping for air and tried to push himself off the ground. He used his crutch for leverage and hauled himself up on his feet. Ryan noticed that behind the door was a large stack of mail, which he realized was the cause of his most immediate troubles. Ryan reached down and collected as much of the mail as he could before limping inside the apartment.

Ryan spent nearly all day going through his mail and throwing out his old, now expired food from his refrigerator. Ryan quickly discerned it was going to cost a fortune to buy more food and a new cell phone. He couldn't imagine hospital bills. As the words twirled around in his mind, Ryan grasped that his hospital bills were lingering, hanging over him, and a slight panic came into the pit of his stomach. He couldn't work like this, so how was he going to make any money to pay them? Ryan began panicking. He had no idea what to do, and he didn't even know how much he owed. Ryan pushed all the letters across his dining room table—they covered nearly the entire thing. Letters of all shapes, sizes, and colors, but one ominous white envelope caught his attention with large red letters stamping "OVERDUE" across the front. Ryan knew this was his hospital bill.

Ryan grabbed the envelope and read the word over and over again. He flipped the envelope and shakily opened it. The bill was extremely long, at least 2 feet. Ryan skipped all the numbers and reached the bottom. He felt very light headed at reading the bill amount due:

Name: Ryan Stark

Account No.: 0118190918

Amount: $188,953.18

Date due: 4/15/2018

Status: Not Paid – OVERDUE

Ryan read this small paragraph over and over. He couldn't believe it, this had to be a joke. Some sick joke played on him. This couldn't possibly be his bill. Ryan was dizzy. He felt like falling out of his chair, he grabbed the table to support himself. He swallowed loudly and felt sick. He was sweating and nervous. What was he going to do? How could he possibly pay this with no income? Ryan was breathing rapidly now. He needed to get a phone and call the hospital. He needed to find out if this was real.

It would have to be the day after though, as Ryan had noticed it was already past midnight. Ryan couldn't believe how much time had passed. He had arrived at his house shortly after 3 o'clock. How was it possibly midnight already? Ryan was stressed and he didn't even feel sleepy, but he had to try.

Ryan grabbed his crutches and an old newspaper and made his way to his bed. He sank onto his bed and set the crutches down near his nightstand. He placed the newspaper in his lap in front of him, on the front page was the accident. Ryan's eyes were transfixed, he began reading the article. It shocked him how much time had already passed.

"Two local residents have been injured in a severe car accident when a distracted driver jumped the divider and struck the car head on. Authorities say both residents were Hannah Fiore, 27, and Ryan Stark, 28. They are both in critical condition."

Ryan stopped reading. He couldn't believe what happened, he never thought it would happen to them, why did they have to suffer? More importantly to Ryan though, why did he have to fight with her? That was the last thing they would ever say to each other…Ryan laid down soon after with his arms outstretched, staring blankly at the ceiling.

CHAPTER 9

Ryan rose to the rising sun, though he didn't remember falling asleep. The sun was streaming into his room now. Ryan was confused by how fast time was passing but he pushed it out of his mind, assuming it was just the stress playing with his mind.

Ryan grabbed his crutches and made his way to his kitchen. He decided to cook eggs, but the correct way, unlike his runny hospital eggs. Ryan opened his fridge only to remember he hadn't gone food shopping, there wasn't anything edible in his fridge. Ryan searched his pantry to find an old box of cereal deep inside The edges of the box were fading. Ryan groaned and scooped out a handful of cereal and chewed on them, they crunched loudly and dried Ryan's mouth out. He downed a few more handfuls of the stale cereal before deciding he should head out to get a new phone. It was necessary for him to have a phone to run his day-to-day life. After Ryan finished his breakfast, he decided to change and leave the house. He called another cab and he was soon off to the store.

Ryan picked out a very generic phone, one that could only call and text. It was about $35.00 and he went to check out. After the cab fares he realized he didn't have enough cash on hand to cover the cost, so he used his credit card. The cashier swiped the card only to have the computer beep loudly and repeatedly. Ryan was confused. The cashier swiped again with the same result.

She turned to face him. "I'm sorry sir, this has been declined," she said.

Ryan stared at the cashier and pulled out another card, which went through the same process.

"Can I just leave it? I'm sorry," Ryan said, his face turning hot pink. Ryan left the store embarrassed and empty handed.

He used the last of his cash to take a cab home. He climbed up the several flights of stairs and realized he had forgotten to check his mailbox. Ryan shrugged it off and made his way to his apartment. There was no way he was struggling back down stairs for more bad news.

Once Ryan entered his apartment, there was a strange envelope on the floor at his feet. It was placed perfectly on the ground facing him with his name written in a neat script handwriting, as if someone entered his apartment and placed it there. Ryan stared at the envelope for a second before picking it up. The envelope was a golden yellow and the writing was in a metallic red ink. It looked as if it came from an inkwell. There was no return address, and as Ryan flipped the envelope over, he found a red wax seal holding it shut. The seal was of a small fox sitting inside of a bed of roses with thorns surrounding it. It was stunning.

Ryan twirled it again and analyzed every aspect of it. The paper was rough, but delicate. The writing was masterfully written, almost like it was printed. Ryan would have assumed it was, if it weren't for a small smudge at the end tail of the 'N' on his name. Ryan sighed and began peeling the wax seal slowly. Once it was off the edge, the envelope sprang open. He pulled the letter out hesitantly. He had never seen such a letter before. It was something a better known person would receive. From the letter fell an envelope already stamped as if someone was expecting a response. Ryan was confused but began to read the letter as he walked to his dining table.

Hello Mr. Stark,

You may not know me. My name is Cornelius Alfred Gray. I am a retired entrepreneur, and I have spent many years building many businesses you may know. I have recently retired to a small house on Rott's Beach.

The reason for this letter is to provide you with the same offer I give to many people in situations like your own. I reach out to several people from towns like Blackridge to give them hope. I have heard your story and I understand the hardship you have experienced. My bargain is this: I will pay for all of your bills and debts. In return I ask that you sell all of your assets and come to Rott's beach to live with me.

I understand your hesitation, for we are strangers, but I can assure you I mean no harm. I am a lonely old man. I have fathered no children and this, I feel, is the best way to use my money and time. To give people who have been broken another chance at life. Of course, you can leave at any time, but know I will not pay for you to leave and you may not return.

Please respond as soon as is convenient for you. I have included an envelope for your convenience. I will send you any further information that you need.

Cordially yours,

Cornelius Alfred Gray

Ryan stared at the letter for a long time. He was puzzled. Why would a total stranger do something so kind? It didn't make any sense to him. Ryan brushed it off and assumed it was a scam. He crumpled up the letter and tossed it aside.

Ryan got up and went into his bedroom. He always tried to prepare for the unexpected, so he had a safe underneath the floorboards in his room. He hadn't asked permission to remove the floorboards from his apartment, but they were already loose, so Ryan took advantage of it. Ryan tried to pick up the safe, but it was extremely heavy for his one arm. He decided to try his best to tip it over, and still he struggled until he thought of an idea. Ryan grabbed his crutches and used one as a lever to push the safe up and out of the floor. Ryan was able to get the safe out but at the cost of bending the crutch leg and rendering it unusable. Ryan threw the crutch in anger, but then he focused on the safe.

Ryan had nearly forgotten the combination, but his fingers moved on their own and opened the safe. Inside was a small cash amount of $200, a silver square watch from a Swiss watchmaker given to him by Hannah, -the battery was dead as the hands of the watch did not move, there was also some family heirlooms. Ryan stared into the safe and realized he had no options. There was no way he could pay for his bills. Ryan pushed the thought from his mind and limped his way to a small box on his nightstand. There was nothing in it besides some coins and old business cards. Ryan pocketed the coins and decided to try to find a payphone.

Ryan left his apartment and searched for a payphone by walking all over town. His legs began to burn from the walking. This was the first time that he had walked more than a few steps without crutches since before the accident. Ryan gasped as he walked. Every step was painful, but he couldn't stop.

Eventually, Ryan found one of the last pay phones in town. It was covered in graffiti and the phone was mostly broken. The sound that emitted from the receiver was mostly static but with the faint trace of a signal. Ryan gathered up the last of his coins and slipped four of them into the machine, which ate them with a happy *clink*. Ryan dialed the operator who eventually directed him to the hospital where he had rested. Ryan had a lump in his throat. He needed to figure out how he could pay the bills without an income.

Through the static came a hoarse voice. "Saint Mary's hospital. How can I help you?"

"Uh-yes. Hi. My name is Ryan Stark. I was a patient at the hospital. I was recently released and I have a past due bill already. Can I pay this in installments?" asked Ryan.

"I'm sorry sir, we do not do any installments of payments. You could take out a loan to cover the upfront cost and pay the loan in monthly installments," cracked the voice over the phone.

"Please, is there any other way? I can't take out a loan of that size. They'll never approve it," pleaded Ryan. The tears returned once more.

"I'm sorry sir, there's nothing I can do. Is there anything else I can help you with?" questioned the voice.

"No," said Ryan softly.

"Okay, thank you and have a nice day." The voice disappeared after a click, and the dial tone returned.

The clink of a returned coin rattled inside Ryan's head for a while before he grabbed it and put it once more into the machine. This time, he called his job. The line rang for several seconds before a familiar male voice answered.

"Hello, Joe Gassi Architecture. How can I help you?" said the gruff voice.

"Joe? It's me, Ryan," said Ryan.

There was a long pause before the voice spoke again.

"Hey, Ryan, what can I do for you?" responded Joe.

"Listen Joe, I've been in a car accident and I need an advance on my next paycheck. I gotta pay off the hospital," said Ryan, hoping there would be a good response.

"I'm sorry to hear about your accident, but I have bad news Ryan. Since you never came back from your vacation, we assumed you forfeited your job. You've been gone for weeks without a call. We waited as long as we could but we had to give your position up," said Joe's gruff voice.

Ryan was floored. He couldn't believe what he was hearing.

"You can't do this to me. I've been loyal to you for years. You can't just throw me to the dogs here," pleaded Ryan once more.

"I don't know what to tell you, Ryan. I can't do anything. I'm sorry," responded Joe with no change in emotion.

"You'll see me in court then! How dare you?" roared Ryan.

"Ryan, it doesn't sound like you can afford a lawyer at this point. I'm sorry but I wish you the best of luck. Goodbye," said John before the click again disconnected Ryan.

"Aaaarrrrgggghhhhh!" Ryan roared and slammed the receiver onto the phone repeatedly until the receiver was knocked out of his hand and dangled in the wind. Ryan placed his hands on the phone and cried into his elbow. Ryan was out of options. He had to accept the stranger's offer.

Ryan returned home and began writing a response letter to the stranger.

Hello Cornelius,

I appreciate your very gracious offer, but you can understand my hesitation when you say I will have to live with you. I am not declining your offer, but I would like more details about the living arrangements with yourself and the other tenants before I can make a decision.

The hospital bills alone total nearly a quarter million dollars, I am not sure your offer will still be on the table if I give you a total of my expenses. Please let me know as much information as you can give me at this time. I need the help.

Thank you for your consideration,

Ryan Stark

Ryan sealed the letter inside the envelope provided by Cornelius. He left the envelope inside the mailbox with the outgoing mail and decided to head to bed. The day had been long and full of disappointments. Ryan was exhausted, but as he lay in bed, the constant reminder of the outstanding bills and debts kept him awake. Ryan swore he saw the clock read 4:50 a.m. before he finally fell asleep.

CHAPTER 10

Several weeks passed and Ryan was finally able to get his cast taken off. His arm felt so weak and vulnerable. He continued to go to physical therapy to help him walk and use his arm again. It was a result of Cornelius' generosity that he was able to continue going to physical therapy, and soon enough he was able to walk on his own with little discomfort. Ryan returned home one day and found another letter in the beautiful handwritten script. It was from Cornelius. He had answered almost all of Ryan's questions and concerns. They had exchanged a few more letters before Ryan felt comfortable making the dreaded decision. After all, Cornelius had already begun to pay off Ryan's debts.

Ryan decided to head out at the end of the month. Cornelius informed him that everything would be taken care of, and he would be picked up promptly at 8 a.m. on the last Thursday of the month at his apartment. Or what would be his old apartment. Ryan had sold everything that had no sentimental meaning to him. He left that apartment with one piece of luggage and a backpack. Nothing but his clothes and some memories disguised as everyday items.

Ryan made a trip to the cemetery before leaving town for the last time, since it was a small town the cemetery was within walking distance of Ryan's apartment. Ryan wondered if he would be able to visit some weekends. The thought of visiting the town he lived in for so many years gave him a strange feeling. Leaves crunched under Ryan's feet as he walked through the squeaky cemetery gates, he felt his heart quicken. When Ryan was a child it seemed strange to him why people would visit cemeteries so often, but now he understood. It was the sense of peace and another chance to talk to the passed, a way to grieve and slowly let go. Ryan walked with a slight limp due to the aches in his leg. He placed a hand on a tombstone and knelt down, he cleared some dead flowers and brush from it.

"Hi mom, I hope you're doing well, things haven't been going so good for me," he said, with his voice breaking. "I wish you were here to help me through this, it hurts all the time, and I wish I could have one of your hugs." Ryan sniffed "I'll try to visit again as soon as I can. I love you mom."

Ryan rose to his feet again, his vision now blurry. He wiped his eyes as best he could, but the tears continued. Ryan let out a shaky breath and continued to walk through the cemetery.

Ryan stopped at a plot that was freshly overturned, there was a small placeholder in lieu of a tombstone. Ryan's legs became weak, and he fell down to his knees. The tears came in long streams with short sobs.

"I don't believe it. I'm so sorry Hannah," cried Ryan. "I wish it was me instead." Ryan placed a hand on the placeholder, it was cold but Ryan couldn't feel it. Ryan's hands were shaking and he felt cold, he sniffed again and raised his eyes to the sky. A crow flew by, cawing. Ryan tried to control his breathing but it was too difficult, his breaths came out jagged and frequent. His chest burned trying to keep the sobs in. Ryan rose again and began to turn away.

"I'm sorry Hannah. I really am," he said as new hot tears flowed over his chilled cheeks. He sniffed and began to walk away.

Over the crunching of leaves, Ryan heard a beeping, he assumed it was a truck backing up somewhere, but he was one of the only people in the cemetery, strange. Ryan shrugged off the noise and walked back to his apartment.

After returned home, Ryan sat on the floor of his now emptied apartment, he stared around the empty room waiting for the intercom to ring. Eventually the intercom buzzed loudly, it was the cab picking him up. Ryan glanced once more around the empty space. It held so many memories. He touched the wall adjacent to him. It was cold, and he could feel tears start to well up, so he decided to make his exit for the last time.

The road to Cornelius' house was bumpy and long. Ryan guessed they must have been driving for well over an hour. Ryan spent most of the time staring at his arm and tracing the outline of a long, jagged scar with his fingers. He could feel the outline, but it was faint. Even with eight weeks of physical therapy, his nerves were still heavily damaged. He looked up and watched the road pass by.

Everything seemed desolate out here. It was just miles and miles of sandy beach. There was a wooden fence running the length of the beach. It gave him a sense of tranquility, reminding him of when he would frequent the beach as a boy. He would walk from the coarse sand by the wooden fenced area to the finer sand made soft by the caress of the ocean waves. Ryan rolled the window down and was immediately hit with the scent of salt water. It was extremely pleasant, and he began to daydream of sitting on the beach with his toes in the sand, watching the tide roll in.

Soon after Ryan drifted into his daydream, the taxi driver rolled the car to a stop and pushed the shifter into park.

"Sir? We've arrived," stated the taxi driver.

Ryan snapped out of his daydream and looked around. He opened the door and the cool breeze immediately hit his body. Ryan shut the door behind him and turned to face what could only be Cornelius' beach house, although Ryan thought that might be the understatement of the year. Ryan was stunned by the size of it. From the letters, Ryan assumed it was a small beach house, but he was very wrong.

It was very large and old. Its paint was faded and worn from years of being bombarded by the ocean mist, slowly eating away at the exterior of the house. The door was slate gray, and the rest of the house was a faded baby blue, like the underside of a glacier. There was a large tower on the right side. It was massive, at least three stories up. Ryan was excited to see the rest of the house. He could see a man standing on the front steps. Ryan slowly limped his way up the stairs to him.

"Hello, my name is—" started Ryan.

"Ryan Stark. I know who you are. We've been expecting you," said the mysterious man in a cool, calm tone. He shook Ryan's hand fiercely, and Ryan winced at his grip. He was an aged man, with the sides of his head slowly fading into a steely grey and a shiny pitch black on top. He was of average height and stature, but his posture was impeccable. He stood up straight and, after shaking Ryan's hand, tucked his hands cleanly behind his back.

"Um, yeah that's me, and you are?" asked Ryan.

"Cornelius Alfred Gray, pleasure to meet you. I am the groundskeeper and the butler, if you will. This is my estate," responded Cornelius.

"Nice to meet you. Do you have a nickname or something? Corny?" chuckled Ryan.

Cornelius' steadfast facial expression did not change. He was very serious, but in a professional manner.

"No," said Cornelius firmly. "You may call me by Cornelius, Alfred, or Mr. Gray. Nothing more, nothing less."

Ryan felt his face grow hot. He didn't want to start off on the wrong foot.

"Right. Well, it's a pleasure to meet you Cornelius," said Ryan.

Cornelius gave a short smile. "Pleasure to meet you as well, sir. Shall I show you around?" Cornelius asked, although he had already turned and began walking inside the house.

Ryan turned to thank the taxi driver but there were only the tire marks in his wake. Ryan saw the luggage he had packed himself beside him. He tried to lift it with his right hand and was again met with sharp pain. He calmly turned and used his left to pick it up. Ryan followed Cornelius through the front door and was met with the stunning interior of the house.

Ryan put down his luggage as he scanned the room in amazement, within the main hall hung several paintings, each of which were different but complementary. The chandelier was dazzling, dividing light into every color of the spectrum onto the walls. There were two large wooden tables on both the right and left sides of the hall with enormous bouquets of flowers and candelabras on each. A very large stairway stood in the center of the room, dividing it in two. At the top of the stairs were the tops of several doors.

"Let me give you the grand tour of the estate," Cornelius began. "This room is the grand hall, or the main entryway, if you will. Upstairs are the bedrooms. I'm sure you are aware of the other tenants," said Cornelius wittingly.

"Uh, no, I was—" Ryan was cut off once again.

"There are seven other tenants, not including myself, of course. All other rooms besides your own are off limits unless you are invited or asked to go in," stated Cornelius firmly. His eyes pierced through Ryan, who suddenly felt fearful of Cornelius.

"Ah, here come one of the tenants now. Ryan, this is Frank," said Cornelius, gesturing toward the man coming down the stairs.

"H-h-hi," said Frank wearily.

"Pleased to meet you. I'm Ryan, the new guy," said Ryan in his most delicate tone.

"Nice to meet you," said Frank quickly, and he scurried out of the grand hall to the right.

"Shall we continue the tour?" said Cornelius, already moving into the next room.

Ryan shuffled quickly to keep up with him. For an older gentleman he moved quickly.

"This is the dining room, where we will eat breakfast, lunch, and dinner, at 9:00 a.m., 2:00 p.m., and 7:00 p.m., respectively. I prefer if you do not miss meal time," said Cornelius.

The dining room was very tasteful. The table was solid mahogany wood with a dark red cherry stain and matching chairs. In the corner was a lovely china cabinet with many glass panels separating beautiful porcelain dishes with intricate floral designs. It reminded him of his mom's old china cabinet. The dining room was attached to a very large kitchen. The refrigerator, which was a large industrial size, was the focal point of the room with several white cabinets surrounding it. In the very center of the room was a large white marble-topped island with a sink and a small refrigerator on the side.

Maybe for drinks?

"Obviously, this is the kitchen. You may choose to come in here and eat or drink whatever you wish at any time of day. One of the few rooms that has no limits at all. Of course, you will clean up after yourself. Every week it is designated to one of the tenants to clean. The refrigerator is always stocked with several different beverages and, of course, food items," Cornelius explained.

Ryan reached over and grabbed the cold steel of the refrigerator's handle. It was much larger on the inside, and the colors were extremely vivid. There were varying shades of color from a deep, sea green to a bright, hot pink. There were vegetables that Ryan wasn't even sure he'd seen before.

On the door of the refrigerator were several shelves filled with different bottles of varying liquids: colas, iced teas, and several homemade concoctions, one of which looked similar to lemonade, but Ryan couldn't be sure.

"If you would like anything, please feel free to help yourself," said Cornelius sternly. He had a twisted look on his face, and Ryan assumed it was due to him opening the refrigerator without asking.

Ryan continued to follow Cornelius through the house. The next room was the living area as Cornelius described. The first thing Ryan noticed were the oversized couches, it looked more like a bed. The recliners were large and also rocked back and forth. The walls were beautifully painted, the floors were hardwood with a dark stain. It was lovely, Ryan had the same idea for a room to be this way when he owned a house. In the middle of the room was a gigantic television set. It had to be at least eighty inches.. Ryan had never seen a television this large, he stood in amazement admiring the set.

"I want you to be as relaxed here as you are at home," said Cornelius with a slight grin.

"So, why do you do this? I mean the house is great and all, but why go through all the trouble? All the spending on such nice things to have people live here for free?" asked Ryan. "You paid for my hospital bills, made me move out of my apartment, and for what?" Ryan heard his voice change slightly.

He didn't mean for it to sound intentionally mean or angry, but it had sounded that way to him. He was feeling confused about what Cornelius's intentions were. None of this made sense.

"Mr. Stark—" started Cornelius.

"Just call me Ryan," said Ryan firmly.

Cornelius breathed a sigh with a small smile. "Ryan, if you are thinking that there is some ulterior motive to what I do, I can assure you that you are wrong," said Cornelius, pausing thoughtfully before he continued. "I wish to help others in need. Each tenant has a past. Each one was broken and attempted to find solace in any way they could. I helped them regain focus and pursue a better life. Not one of the tenants has left since I took them in."

Cornelius had an expression on his face that resembled sadness, as if he had personally gone through a traumatic experience getting them here.

"Yeah, well, they don't pay for anything, so of course they won't leave," said Ryan mockingly.

"Some people take advantage of our kindness, but that does not mean we should not offer it. Everyone has a story, their own tragedies, their own struggles. Kindness is sometimes the key to moving forward," said Cornelius flatly. Cornelius turned and began to walk out of the room.

Ryan still felt hot from the discussion and wanted to pursue it further, but it was clear Cornelius wasn't going to give in. Ryan hesitated but soon pursued. He didn't understand why Cornelius would do this for a complete stranger.

Cornelius stopped in front of two large glass sliding doors, but Ryan couldn't see out of them. The sun had already faded away and the moon had begun to rise. It was cloudy and the moon provided only a dim light. There was a mat on the floor with several pairs of shoes tossed about. Ryan wondered if this was a back entrance to the house.

"And last, but not least, this is my favorite portion of the tour. Be sure to take off your shoes here," said Cornelius as he began untying his dress shoes. Ryan didn't want any more altercations with Cornelius, and so he slipped off his sneakers.

Cornelius grasped the handles of the sliding doors and gently pulled them away from each other. As he opened the door, Ryan was hit once again with a wave of the scents of the familiar ocean breeze. Both Cornelius and Ryan closed their eyes and slowly breathed in the salty air. Ryan heard the clicking of light switches that forced him to open his eyes, his concentration broken. The patio lights flickered on and off before finally staying on. The patio was illuminated, and Ryan could see much clearer. This was also his favorite part of the tour.

Ryan quickly took off his socks before stepping out onto the wooden deck. The wood was old, worn by years of enjoyment and the ocean mist that had slowly degraded and warped its structure. The wood was cold, but the atmosphere was warm and inviting. Ryan looked around and the deck was the most modest part of the house. From the outside, it was as if Cornelius had only enough money to feed himself, let alone seven other people.

There were a few lawn chairs scattered about, and a small, worn down plastic table that bore scratches and burn marks. There was a half-full ashtray left near the edge of the table and an empty cooler nearby that was missing the top. The deck also had stairs leading directly onto the beach. Ryan could hear the gentle lapping of the ocean waves hitting the shore.

"I spend most of my time out here relaxing and taking in the sights. If you ever require my assistance, check here first," said Cornelius as he stared off into the distance.

"I'm sure you'll be seeing me here most of the time too," said Ryan, smiling.

Cornelius nodded slightly. "Well, that concludes the tour. Your luggage is already in your room. Feel free to change and shower if you would like before dinner. It will be served at 7:00 sharp, so you have an hour," said Cornelius.

Ryan looked down beside himself confused, he didn't remember leaving his luggage behind. Cornelius was already beginning to walk away when Ryan looked up.

"Uh, listen. Thank you, for all of this," Ryan started, motioning around with his hands. "I'm sorry if I came off like an ass earlier. I've just never had anyone do me any favors before," Ryan finished, blushing.

"It is quite alright. I understand," said Cornelius, keeping his focus on the invisible ocean. He had never once turned to face Ryan since they had come out here.

"Well, follow me, and I will show you up to your room," said Cornelius as he waved his arm to direct Ryan back inside.

They returned to the large entranceway. It was still ever so large compared to the rest of the house. Cornelius started up the stairs.

They made their way down the small hallway, passing several doors with names etched into them. One by one they passed, and Ryan glanced briefly at the names: Frank—the tenant he had met in the hall—James, Jamie, Anzo, Daniella, Sam, and Greg, until finally they reached

Ryan's. Next to his were another two doors, one at the end of the hall and the other right next to his. Cornelius didn't bother to explain what they were.

Cornelius slipped a brass key into the keyhole and unlocked Ryan's door. He pushed open the door and waited with his arm outstretched to let Ryan in. Ryan glanced around the room. To his right was a small, dark brown wooden desk, which had seen its fair share of use. On the desk was a lamp and some papers with pens scattered about as if it had been recently used. The bathroom was directly in front of the door they entered and on the left was Ryan's bed and a large dresser. On the bed was his luggage, waiting. It was not a special room by any means, but it felt like his old room at his parent's house. It was warm and calm inside.

"Here's your key. It will only open your door. We are not allowed inside another person's room without permission and if I catch you, you will be asked to leave immediately," said Cornelius sternly.

"I understand," said Ryan calmly, facing Cornelius. Then Ryan turned and faced the room, taking everything in.

"I know it's not my place to ask," said Ryan, fiddling and turning the key over in his hands. The base of the key was etched with complicated designs. "But what are the other two rooms next to mine?" he finally asked.

There was no response. He turned around. Cornelius was nowhere to be found and Ryan's door was closed.

Ryan opened his door and looked out into the corridor but couldn't find Cornelius. Ryan reluctantly left his room. Ryan crept along the wall until he hit a doorway, he presumed to be the one right next to his room. He peered over and looked at the name etched onto the door, but it was unreadable aside from an uppercase L. It was crossed out several times with deep, uneven cuts. Ryan glossed over the scratches with his fingers. The wood was deeply separated. The knife used must have been very sharp.

What the hell? Ryan whispered as his fingers rasped against the broken wood. Ryan looked at the door to the left at the end of the hallway. The name etched into the door was painted with a golden, glossy paint. It was very elegant and, of course, Ryan figured that this was the door leading to Cornelius' room. The door stood out from the rest. It was made of a heavy, dark wood with intricately carved door handles while the other rooms had plain, light brown doors with mundane brass handles. It was expected for a house this age, but Cornelius' room was clearly renovated to match his persona.

Ryan turned to make his way back to his room. However, a man was now standing between him and his room. The man had jet black hair and dark colored eyes.

The man was attempting to look inside Ryan's room as the door was slightly cracked open.

"Can I help you?" Ryan said, obviously annoyed.

"So, you're the new tenant?" asked the man. He scoffed and crossed his arms. "Seems as though they'll let anyone in here nowadays," he continued, looking at Ryan like he was nothing more than a rat.

"Right, well I'm here. So, you can deal with it or you can leave," snapped Ryan.

The man's expression turned dark, the calm look on his face now angry. He moved closer to Ryan until Ryan could feel the man's warm breath when he spoke.

"You better watch your step. It's a long fall to the bottom," said the man, staring straight into Ryan's eyes. Ryan's anger soon washed away, and he was left feeling intimidated and somewhat scared.

"Leave him alone, Anzo. You were once the new guy too," said a familiar voice.

Ryan inched over to see who the voice belonged to. It was Frank.

Anzo turned around and laughed. "And you're going to do something about it? Yeah, right." He turned once more to face Ryan and gave him a glaring look. He looked at the room once more and turned toward Frank. He walked right past him, but not before using his shoulder to push Frank into the wall. Frank looked as if he'd expected it. Clearly it was a usual occurrence.

"You alright?" asked Frank.

"Ye-yeah, I'll be alright," Ryan sputtered, his anger now turning into fear. Ryan felt nauseous. "I should go unpack my stuff, so...." Ryan looked toward his door.

Frank looked at him and nodded before turning toward the staircase and retreating down the steps. Ryan pushed his door fully open and entered. He closed the door and locked it behind him. He wasn't afraid of the other tenants, it just gave him a sense of comfort to be behind a locked door. It always had.

Ryan faced his luggage and unzipped it. He took out his clothes and placed them in the dresser near his bed. Once all of his clothes were removed from his bag, he placed it behind the door and returned to his backpack. He opened it and right on top was a black box. Inside the box was the jewel that Hannah had given him. Ryan stroked the corners of the box and went to open it. He hesitated as a surge of memories come back to him. He could see Hannah on the mountain they had hiked, her glowing face with her hair wild in the wind. Her tight ponytail as they were driving. And then his memories turned dark. He saw Hannah's face bloodied and bruised after the accident, then Hannah in the hospital with tubes coming and going in all different directions.

Ryan took a short breath and wiped tears from his face. He stopped opening the box and placed it on the bed, covering it with his hand. Just looking at it made him feel sad. He stared inside the backpack until he heard something outside his door. Ryan sniffled and wiped his eyes before slowly making his way to the door. He stepped slowly and lightly as to not make any noise. The floorboards were hardwood and very old. He did not want them giving him away.

Ryan eventually reached his door and kneeled in front of it. He stared out of the keyhole before coming within what seemed like millimeters of a bright blue eye staring right back at him. Ryan leaped back in fear. When he looked back, the mysterious eye had disappeared. If Ryan hadn't heard footsteps running quickly from his door to another door before a loud slam, he might not have thought it was real. Ryan sat on the floor, confused. He pondered who would want to spy on him through the keyhole. Ryan figured it would be best to avoid this situation again. He got up off the floor and pulled the brass key from his pocket and slid it into the keyhole. Ryan then returned to unpacking his things. His backpack was soon empty, and just before he put it next to his luggage, Ryan placed the box back inside his backpack. He decided some things were better left unopened. Ryan laid on the bed and his arm weighed a ton, the scar burned and ached, he was glad to finally rest.

CHAPTER 11

Ryan awoke to the sunshine streaming in through the small curtains above his bed. He had fallen asleep in his clothes from last night. He flickered his eyes open but laid in bed staring at the ceiling, there was a knock at the door.

"Breakfast in fifteen minutes!" Said the voice, it was muffled but Ryan believed it to be the voice of Cornelius. He only had fifteen minutes to freshen up before heading down. Ryan wondered what Cornelius would do if he showed up late.

Ryan headed to his private bathroom. He realized only now that his shower was quite grand. Stainless steel door handles, glass shower doors, and small aquamarine tiles. He noticed the whole bathroom was quite luxurious, it was identical to something he had once seen in a home design magazine. He quickly changed his shirt and splashed cold water on his face. He looked at himself in the mirror and really hated what he saw staring back at him.

He could barely recognize himself. His face had a long scar going through his eyebrow and a few smaller scars on his cheek and chin. Ryan's black hair now grew long and began to make its way into Ryan's eyes. Nevertheless, Ryan exited the room and bumped into another tenant as he did so, a dark skinned slender man with long shaggy hair.

"Oh sorry didn't see you there," said Ryan

"Yeah, most people don't now, I'm not the new guy anymore," replied the man.

Ryan was slightly taken aback

"I'm Ryan by the way," he said opening his hand to the stranger

"James," said the man quietly as he walked away

Dick thought Ryan, but the man was halfway down the stairs when he gave a backwards glance to Ryan, which caused him to think, did he hear him?

Ryan soon headed downstairs toward the kitchen where he saw Cornelius in a navy suit and tie with an apron wrapped around him. It made Ryan chuckle. It wasn't every day you saw a man in a suit and an apron. He scanned the room to see many unfamiliar faces, most of whom were not very keen to introduce themselves or even make eye contact with Ryan. He felt like an outcast to the other tenants, almost as if he didn't understand them and vice-versa. He quickly pushed the thought of meeting the other tenants out of his mind. The smells that filled the room were overwhelming: sizzling bacon, French vanilla coffee, fresh fruit, ocean mist, frying eggs, and it all seemed like a dream. A perfect breakfast in a perfect setting.

"Good morning, Ryan!" said Cornelius.

"Good morning, Cornelius," Ryan returned with a smile. Ryan quickly spotted Frank outside and decided to join him. There was a sliding door that led to yet another porch, this one facing the beach but not quite on it. Frank turned with a jump at the sight of Ryan.

"Oh, I'm sorry. I didn't mean to startle you," said Ryan apologetically.

"It's quite alright. I'm used to it by now," said Frank, running his hands through his hair.

Ryan could now see the ocean and it was beautiful. The ocean mist quickly filled Ryan's nose while the sounds of seagulls and crashing waves filled his ears. He could taste the salt of the ocean and could feel the cool ocean breeze. Ryan closed his eyes to fully embrace the ocean's salty, crisp grip.

"Don't you just love the ocean?" asked Ryan. He opened his eyes and turned to Frank, but Frank was visibly shaking, his fingers fidgeting like he was afraid of something.

"Yeah, it's lovely," said Frank in a flat tone. Ryan could see his discomfort and he did not pursue conversation any longer.

"The time is now 9:00 a.m. Please come in and join us," said Cornelius, poking his head out of the sliding door.

Ryan and Frank turned and made their way inside. They followed Cornelius into the dining room. Once there Ryan almost couldn't believe his eyes. The table was barely visible and was covered with a breakfast feast: an entire stack of bacon, four different kinds of eggs, ham, breads, muffins, several different drinks such as orange juice, grapefruit juice, coffee, milk, tea, lemonade, and several sides of cut fruit. Ryan was amazed at everything he saw. "W-wow. You made all of this?" asked Ryan.

"Yes, sir. I make breakfast, lunch, and dinner each and every day for all of the tenants," responded Cornelius with a short, tight smile. He quickly resumed his normal disposition.

Ryan could feel his mouth filling with saliva. He hadn't realized it, but he was starving. His stomach was hurting, and he couldn't wait to eat. Ryan looked around the table and saw several people he didn't recognize. Only Anzo, Frank, and Cornelius were familiar.

Cornelius was the first to speak. "Everyone, may I have your attention please? I would like to introduce our newest tenant," said Cornelius. "This is Ryan Stark. I expect you to give him a warm welcome," said Cornelius in his stern voice. His gaze was very sharp and pierced the other tenants.

Everyone around the table gave a Ryan a look before giving him a quick greeting. They all seemed scared, possibly from Cornelius's stern gaze.

After breakfast, Ryan began to clean up his own dishes. He was stopped by an unfamiliar voice.

"Hey, new guy. What was your name again?"

Ryan looked up and saw a light skinned blonde woman with bright green eyes staring back at him.

"Uh, it's Ryan," he replied, caught off guard. "And you are?"

"Oh, sorry. I figured you would've heard about me already. I'm Amy," said Amy, flipping her hair behind her ear in a way that Ryan was sure she thought would flatter him, but Ryan found her attitude annoying and arrogant. "You know we don't do the dishes around here right? Cornelius does everything for us. Most people notice that by now," said Amy.

"What do you—" Before Ryan could finish his sentence, Cornelius appeared in the doorway.

"Amy. I see you have met Mr. Stark. I hate to break up this gathering, but isn't there something else you should be doing?" questioned Cornelius. He shot her a quick gaze that caused her to look away.

"Yes, sir," said Amy quietly. She turned and exited the room without looking up.

"You'll find that there are some people here that would be in your best interest to limit conversation with," said Cornelius sternly. He looked at Ryan with his bright blue eyes, and Ryan felt the gaze piercing into him. This tactic reminded Ryan of his own mother, the thought of her disapproving gaze was enough to make Ryan shudder.

"Right, I'll keep that in mind, thanks," said Ryan hesitantly. Ryan turned to pick up his dishes when Cornelius grabbed his plates from him.

"Don't worry about those, I can handle this from here. You just relax and get to know the other tenants or explore the house or property. The beach should be lovely at this time," said Cornelius. He gave a quick, small grin.

"Okay, yeah, sure. Thanks," said Ryan. He couldn't understand why Cornelius refused his help. It was strange but he didn't question it.

Ryan went to the fridge and grabbed a water bottle. He decided to take a walk on the beach to try and clear his head. He checked his pockets to make sure he had his room key and left the house.

Once outside, Ryan felt a blast of cool ocean breeze. That, along with the sun shining on his face, made him extremely comfortable. Ryan headed down the stairs off the porch and took off his shoes and socks. He placed his shoes on the stairwell and dug his feet into the warm sand. Ryan began to walk toward the tide and the cool ocean swept over his ankles. Ryan closed his eyes and took a deep breath.

Ryan felt very peaceful and, though he hated swimming, the thought of taking a dip in the cool ocean water really appealed to him. Ryan pushed the thought out of his mind and began walking alongside the tide, the wet sand leaving footprints in his wake.

Ryan began to let his mind wander, and his thoughts drifted to Hannah. She loved the beach and often tried to get Ryan to join her. Ryan disliked the idea of sweating in the sweltering heat and having the problem of sand getting in all different areas. Hannah loved the beach for all of its unique beauties: the shells that could be found, the aquatic animals, the sand between her toes, and the sun bouncing off her shimmering, flowing hair.

Ryan continued on his way, feeling nostalgic but also sad, like a rock in his stomach. Ryan could feel a wave of sadness crashing inside him. It shattered his soul and reverberated up his spine. Ryan could feel tears forming, but he quickly wiped them away when he heard a voice calling out to him.

"Hey, new guy!" said yet another woman. She had very long flowing hair, light hazel eyes, tan skin, and freckles.

Ryan felt uncomfortable. he didn't want her to see him crying, and he sniffed. "Yes? Who are you?" said Ryan, trying to keep his voice firm.

"My name's Sam! I'm one of the other tenants," said Sam.

"Oh…alright. Well, nice meeting you," said Ryan, returning to his walk.

"Mind if I join you?" asked Sam.

Ryan hesitated. He really didn't want to have any company on his walk, but he didn't want to give her a bad impression. After all, he would probably be here a while.

"Sure," said Ryan.

Ryan couldn't help but look at Sam, watching her walk along the sand. She had on a bikini top and some cutoff jeans. She held her sandals in one hand and used the other to try and keep her hair out of her face. Ryan couldn't look away from her body.

"You see something you like?" questioned Sam.

"Oh, um," said Ryan, now blushing bright red.

"Sorry, it's just been a while since I've seen a woman," said Ryan, now blushing even harder.

"Oh. Well, there's nothing to worry about. I'm happy with showing off my body," said Sam, winking. "So you can stop blushing now." Sam smiled and bit her lip.

Ryan couldn't stop blushing.

"So, what brings you here?" asked Sam, more serious now.

"I uh," Ryan hesitated, he felt tears welling up and stopped to take a breath.

"I was in a car accident, got hurt pretty bad...Cornelius offered to help me," responded Ryan hoping to divert her attention back to Cornelius.

"Yeah, Cornelius is nice like that. He rescued me, too," said Sam, now looking down at her feet.

"What happened? I-if you don't mind my asking," said Ryan, now seeing Sam's scrunched face.

"I don't mind. I tried to kill myself. I lost my parents and I felt as if I had lost everything. I was homeless until Cornelius found me. He saved my life," said Sam with her voice quivering.

Ryan looked away. He decided that staring at her would make her uncomfortable. Ryan felt something strange—even though he had just met her, he felt sorry and sad for her. He wanted to give her what she wanted, but he didn't know how.

"It's getting late. Should we turn around?" asked Sam.

Ryan looked around and it was well past midday. Time had moved so fast he hadn't even realized that it was already time for lunch.

"Oh, yeah. Wouldn't want to keep Cornelius waiting," said Ryan with a smirk.

The two turned around and began to head back to the house. Their footprints fading away in their wake.

Both Sam and Ryan had returned to the house with time to spare before lunch. The two entered through the sliding door next to the kitchen, and in the kitchen was Cornelius in his apron by the stove. Sam brushed her feet off and began to walk through the house.

"There you two are. Enjoying your time?" asked Cornelius, now facing them.

"Yeah, lovely," said Sam, walking past Cornelius. She turned her head over her shoulder to give a quick look at Ryan before exiting the room.

"Little devil that one," said Cornelius, peering at the empty doorway through his small glasses. Ryan assumed he wore them to be able to read the recipe book that was ajar near the stove. "Well, better hurry Ryan. Lunch will be ready soon," said Cornelius, turning back to the stove.

Ryan nodded, but in his mind, he didn't understand how the time had passed so quickly, it felt as though he just ate breakfast a few minutes ago. He brushed his feet on the mat and walked through the room. Ryan headed up the stairs toward his room. He passed by Sam's room and swore he could hear crying…. Ryan put it out of his mind and decided it was best to give her space. When Ryan reached his door, there was a small package wrapped in brown paper with a note on it.

Hope this will help you. Use it as a diary or a place to vent. Sometimes paper can be more useful than a friendly ear.

Regards-

Cornelius

Ryan took his key out of his pocket and opened his room door, still staring at the package. Once inside, he placed the package on his bed. He shut his door and sat on his bed. He pulled the package onto his lap and began to open it. Inside was a leather-bound journal. It was faintly reminiscent of one he had as a child, given to him by his father. Ryan was instructed on writing his thoughts down instead of talking about them. It left a pit in his stomach remembering it. On the outside of the journal the initials RS were burned into the cover, and the journal was bound by two leather straps and tied in a knot on the front.

Underneath the journal was a long, thin, cardboard box. Ryan turned the box over and heard a rattle. He turned the box back over and opened it. Inside was a heavy metal pen. It was very elegant, it was engraved with all kinds of markings, Ryan noticed a ladybug somewhere in the mix, but it strained his eyes to look so intently. Ryan picked up the pen. It felt cold in his hands, but it was well balanced and felt like an extension of Ryan himself.

Ryan laughed to himself. It was a nice gesture, but Ryan couldn't keep up with all the nice things Cornelius was doing for him. Ryan wanted to think of a way to repay him, but couldn't yet figure out how. Ryan placed the book and pen on the bed beside him. He got clean clothes out of his dresser and took off his old, sweaty clothing. He tossed his used clothing into a hamper near the door when he saw the leather box poking out of his backpack. Ryan stared at it as it ached in his heart. He tried not to think of Hannah, but like an instinct, he could feel it. Ryan was confused why it would be poking out, it shouldn't have been anywhere near the top. Ryan got up and pushed it back inside and zipped it closed.

Ryan hesitated, but eventually put it out of his mind. He started the shower and waited for it to heat up. Once ready, Ryan got into the shower and spent a good ten minutes pondering, the hot water wrapping around him like a fluid blanket, the steam filling his nose and mouth. Once he finished, Ryan stepped outside. The difference in temperature awakened his senses, the cold tightening his skin and attacking his throat and nose. Ryan put on his clothing and began to head downstairs.

Ryan opened his door to leave, but a thought came to his mind. Ryan closed the door, he rested his hand on the doorknob and hesitated before he reached back around to his bag and unzipped it. He picked up the box inside the bag and ran his fingers along its corners again. The broken leather revealed the wood underneath, rubbing the edges comforted him until the scar on his arm began aching. Ryan placed his hand on it, he felt it pulse underneath his fingers. He looked around before deciding to place the box in his dresser under his clothing. Ryan let out a sigh and exited the room.

Coming down the stairs, the smell of fresh grilled vegetables and sauces filled his nose. Like a switch, Ryan's stomach started hurting and gurgling. Ryan was eager to see what Cornelius had prepared. Ryan walked quickly through the dining room and turned into the doorway and, to his surprise, Cornelius was not in the kitchen. He turned back toward the dining room and the table was half set up, but no one was around. Ryan was confused. Suddenly, Ryan heard a loud thud from upstairs. It came more from the stairway.

Ryan's heart beat a little faster. He took a deep breath and began walking back toward the stairway. Ryan kept his right hand on the wall parallel to him. He came out to the open stairway clearing and he let his body relax a little. Nothing was out of the ordinary so far. Ryan began to head up the stairs and toward his room once more. The only rooms past his were Cornelius' and the mystery room. Just as Ryan reached his door, Cornelius opened his door. Both Ryan and Cornelius were startled by the other's presence.

"Oh, sorry. I didn't mean to scare you," said Ryan.

"Oh, don't worry about that. You just about ready for lunch?" said Cornelius. He was fumbling a lot, as he dropped the handkerchief he was using to wipe his hands. Ryan looked away from him but the thud from earlier still rang in his mind. Ryan wanted to push his luck and see what information he could get.

"Sorry, sir, but when I was downstairs I heard something of a thud. Do you know anything about it?" asked Ryan, trying not to show his deep curiosity.

"Oh, I wouldn't know. I was in my bathroom," said Cornelius, stuffing his handkerchief away.

Strange. Why wouldn't he use a towel to wipe his hands?

"You said you heard a thud? As if someone fell? I should probably check this out," said Cornelius. "Oh, Ryan, could you go downstairs and check the pot? Thank you," said Cornelius as he walked away.

Well I guess this is one way to repay him.

Ryan headed back downstairs to the stove. Ryan picked up a wooden spoon on the counter and stirred the contents of the pot. A smell of basil and onions wafted to his nose, and it smelled delicious. Cornelius soon appeared in the doorway.

"Well, it doesn't look like anyone fell or got hurt, so I'm not sure what you heard," said Cornelius.

Ryan was confused. He didn't usually hear things that didn't happen.

"May I?" said Cornelius, gesturing to the spoon in Ryan's hand.

"Oh, yeah, sure," Ryan said, realizing what he meant.

"Lunch should be ready in ten minutes. Would you mind finishing setting the table, Ryan?" asked Cornelius. "Just need to add the utensils."

"Sure, where is everything?"

"The drawer to the left of the fridge has the forks, spoons, and knives. The cabinet above that has plates, and napkins are over here to my left," said Cornelius, pointing to a small box full of napkins.

Ryan opened the drawer and grabbed a handful of forks and knives before he decided he didn't know what was needed.

"So, what are we eating?" asked Ryan quietly. "So I know what to grab and put on the table."

Cornelius looked over at him. "Spoons and a knife should be fine. We are eating stew," replied Cornelius.

Ryan replaced the forks he had picked up and instead grabbed a handful of spoons, Ryan was anxious to begin the meal, stew was one of Ryan's favorite dishes. He could feel his stomach grumbling at the very smell of it. It was odd though, he felt hungry, but at the same time, he didn't want to eat, it was difficult to put the mystery of the thud away. Once lunch was served, Ryan grabbed a seat at the table. The dining table was filled with all sorts of delectable foods: different kinds of breads, condiments, and spices lay about, and there were several drinks to choose from. The table itself was barely large enough to hold it all.

Ryan again took in the sight and marveled at Cornelius' generosity. He was happy to be a part of his tenant group, but Ryan could find himself getting comfortable. Ryan glanced around the table and noticed something odd, at dinner last night and breakfast this morning, all the chairs were filled. However, now there was one seat empty. Ryan felt a little awkward, as he hadn't met everyone, so he couldn't have a definitive reason for someone to be missing but he wouldn't let his pessimism get to him. Could this be the thud he heard? Had someone perished in this house? Ryan couldn't see a reason for it.

Ryan pushed any other thoughts out of his mind and decided to focus on the delicious lunch. There was chatter in the air between tenants, but no one talked to Ryan. Not that he minded, though. Ryan liked to keep to himself, especially in social situations. Instead, Ryan tried to keep a visual log of everyone at the table, He decided that if anyone else disappeared, hopefully this time around he could see who and why they could've gone. Once Ryan had finished with lunch, he again offered to help Cornelius clean up the dishes.

"Nonsense, you shouldn't have to worry about such things," said Cornelius.

Ryan again didn't argue and instead decided to return to his room. He left the room and returned to the main hall and began up the stairs. Once Ryan reached the top, a thought struck him. Instead of making a usual left toward his room, Ryan turned right, checking over his shoulder to make sure no one had seen him make the incorrect direction change. Ryan walked all the way down the hall. The last door at the end of the hallway showed exactly what Ryan believed. The name of the tenant that used to reside there was scratched out with deep markings. Ryan felt his stomach sink and his heart beat faster. Ryan raised a shaky hand toward the doorknob, and his fingers were just about to grasp it when he was startled by a voice.

"You shouldn't do that," said a familiar voice.

Ryan turned and found Frank standing between him and the open hallway.

"Oh, I was just—" But before Ryan could finish his thought, Frank cut him off.

"I understand what you're doing, but don't. You don't understand things yet, and it's too dangerous to wander around like this. Do yourself a favor and mind your own business or it could end poorly," said Frank. His face still had the worried look Ryan had seen before, but his voice was stern.

Ryan turned his gaze back to the doorknob. He took his hand and lowered it. Ryan looked up and saw that Frank was gone. In his wake, a door slammed shut.

Ryan began walking toward his room and saw the name "Frank" sketched into the door next to the staircase. There were several other doors with tenants' names, but

Ryan decided not to check them all. As Frank had said, he should keep to himself.

Ryan returned to his room and lay down on his bed. While it was nice to be here, it was quite boring. Ryan quickly found himself staring at the ceiling for almost an hour.

"This is ridiculous. I'm going to die if I just sit and wait here," said Ryan. He swung his legs off the edge of the bed. He decided to explore the house more and maybe find something to do. Ryan left his room, locked his door and began down the stairs.

Let's see…. Through the kitchen to the living room?

He couldn't believe he'd already forgotten where everything was. Ryan walked through the dining room, now adorned with empty chairs and an empty table. Ryan walked past the room and through the kitchen. The sink was spotless, and Ryan was shocked at how quickly Cornelius cleaned everything up.

Ryan looked around for a clock but noticed none near him. He actually didn't even remember seeing any clocks when he arrived. Ryan was confused, but he didn't really care much for hunting down clocks. He continued on and finally found his way into the living room. The fire was roaring in the fireplace but no one was around. Maybe Cornelius left it going as a comfort for the other tenants, but Ryan would save the question for Cornelius the next time he saw him.

Ryan walked by a table with a lamp on it. In passing, Ryan could have sworn he saw a picture of his parents, so much that he stopped in his tracks. Ryan turned and picked up the frame, but when he studied the picture, it was just of Cornelius and another tenant. Bizarre.

Ryan placed the picture back on the table and continued to the bookshelf, gazing at the spines of the books. Nothing really stood out at Ryan, but he decided to pick up a random book. It wasn't titled and gave no indication of an author, it looked more like a journal than a written illustration. He took the book to the nearest chair and sat. The leather seat groaned under Ryan. It was old but very comfortable.

As Ryan opened the book, the spine cracked under his hands and a smell of old paper wafted through his nose. The book felt very old but it seemed like it was never opened. Ryan flipped to the to the first page and, as he began reading, he understood that the book was written by someone, it was a memoir of sorts. Ryan continued to read the memories of another person, but they seemed very familiar to Ryan. Ryan read the pages and saw the similarity between himself and the mysterious author. The story of a man napping in a hammock at his parents' house with the family dog resting near him rang around in Ryan's head. He could've sworn that this was an exact replica of his past. Ryan distinctly remembered this memory, and he became increasingly uncomfortable. How can someone have the same experiences as his life and who was this mystery author? Was it…Cornelius?

No, it's not possible.

Ryan had never seen Cornelius before the other day. There was no way he could be in all the same places as him. Ryan pushed the thought out of his mind as best he could, it was possible for multiple people to have the same experiences, it had to be coincidence. Ryan slammed the book shut and returned it to the shelf. He picked up another book and read it. Again, it had a memory that was similar to Ryan's. He closed it and picked up a new one. Another memory Ryan had experienced. Ryan was sweating. He was nervous and confused at the same time. How many stories were there?

Ryan looked up at the shelf and there were dozens of books. Ryan assumed they were all in the same vein. Ryan put his hand to his chin and stroked it, he couldn't believe how many volumes there were, and from behind him a voice startled him.

"Something wrong?" said the voice. Ryan turned around and saw Anzo with a woman next to him.

"Do all of you people just like sneaking around?" asked Ryan angrily.

Anzo snorted. "Don't flatter yourself. It's bound to happen when people live together," said Anzo. "So, what's up?"

Ryan sneered. "Why do you care?" he snarled.

"Ouch, so sassy," said the woman.

Anzo snorted again. Ryan was annoyed with him and he wanted to leave, but he almost felt jealous of Anzo. He wanted to make friends with the other tenants, but he found it difficult.

"And who are you?" asked Ryan. He could feel the anger building in his voice.

"Jamie. Pleasure to meet you. Can I see that book?" asked Jamie.

"No…. I'm using it," replied Ryan, clutching the book close to his chest.

The woman laughed. "Okay, I'll just get my own," said Jamie. She grabbed a random book off the shelf and motioned to Anzo as they both began to leave the room.

Ryan knew he didn't own any of the books, but yet he still felt bitter and jealous of her taking it. Ryan glared at them but said nothing.

As the pair were leaving, Anzo put his hand on the doorframe and looked over his shoulder at Ryan. "You know, those 'diaries' are writings of Cornelius. You might want to talk to him if you're interested in them," said Anzo. He clicked his tongue and left the room.

Ryan looked back at the book in his hands. So many books and none of them have names or dates. Does he just make them and store them? Ryan was curious, but he wasn't sure if he should go talk to Cornelius about it yet. He placed the book back on the shelf and stepped back to take a look at the library.

Ryan tried to push it out of his mind. Anzo was trying to get under Ryan's skin. The problem was, he was succeeding. Ryan sat back down on the recliner. He couldn't figure out why those memories were so familiar to him. Ryan's eyes felt heavy, the fire was crackling, and the warmth of it lulled his eyes closed. He took a deep breath and let it out slow. Ryan shook the sleepiness off and decided to head to his room, there was much to do.

Ryan sat on the edge of his bed with a book from the library, opened to a page with a very specific memory on it. Ryan kept reading the lines over and over again, trying to make sense of them. There was a sort of eerie nervousness in his stomach. Ryan just couldn't believe what he was reading, a memory which he thought could only happen to him. It was possible that someone else had a memory the same as him, like a kid eating an ice pop on the fourth of July or a first dip in a creek. This memory though, with this attention to detail…it was as if someone had reached into the back of Ryan's mind and placed the extracts on paper.

Ryan assumed it was almost time for dinner. Ryan dog eared the page of the book and shut it. Ryan got up to leave, but figured it'd be best to hide the book from prying eyes, even though he locked his door every time he stepped out.

Ryan hid the book under his pillow, easy enough not to be found by anyone and easy to tell if it was moved. Ryan stepped out of his room and locked his door. As Ryan began down the stairs, he felt someone watching him. Ryan turned to face the opposite hall, and as he did, a door slammed shut.

Strange.

Seeing as he was running out of time, he decided to just head down to the kitchen, after double-checking his door was locked, of course. After another delicious meal, Ryan decided to stay in his seat this time around. After the other tenants had left, Ryan tried to question Cornelius about the books in the library

Unfortunately, Cornelius moved swiftly to clear the table in less than ten minutes. Ryan was stunned to see how quickly the table had been cleared, but nonetheless, he was determined to get an answer.

Ryan raised himself out of his seat and pushed in his chair slowly. Ryan left his hands on the back of the chair. The fabric was comforting under Ryan's fingertips. After Cornelius had picked up the last plate and glass, Ryan followed him out of the room.

"Hey, Cornelius?" said Ryan in a quiet voice.

"Hm?" hummed Cornelius.

"I have a question for you," said Ryan kindly.

"Ask away," said Cornelius with a quick, short smile.

"Well, I was wondering about those books in your library," said Ryan nervously.

Cornelius stopped washing the dishes. He turned to look over his shoulder. He looked worried.

"What about it?" said Cornelius.

"Well, I just happened to notice that the memoirs in those books are strangely similar to memories I had of my childhood. Can I ask where these memoirs came from?" asked Ryan, slightly more confident.

Cornelius's expression changed. He seemed almost relieved. Ryan was confused but intrigued.

"They are not actually my memoirs. See, when tenants move in, I ask them each to write down a memory where they felt their very best, in control and powerful," said Cornelius. "I have collected them over the years, and they have been stacked on that library wall ever since. I am not sure anyone ever actually read them," said Cornelius.

Ryan was thoroughly confused now. Anzo had told him to ask Cornelius, but it turned out the tenants wrote the books? It didn't make any sense.

"Oh, I see. Well, thanks for telling me," said Ryan with a small smirk. "Well, I think that's all I've got. I guess I should head back to my room."

"Alright. Well, have a good night, Ryan," said Cornelius.

"Thanks, you too," said Ryan.

CHAPTER 12

Cornelius watched Ryan leave out of the corner of his eye. He pretended to wash the dish in his hand. Once Ryan left and his footsteps retreated up the stairs, Cornelius turned around and saw Anzo coming back to the kitchen from the porch.

"What did you say to him?" hissed Cornelius.

"Relax, boss. Nothing he shouldn't have known anyway," responded Anzo.

"Are you a fool!" said Cornelius angrily.

"What do you mean? I'm trying to help," said Anzo.

Cornelius was steadily approaching Anzo. Anzo reached behind him to grab the counter top.

"Dude, stay away," said Anzo,

"You're going to ruin everything! I can't have you do that!" screeched Cornelius. He pulled out a red hilted blade. It gleamed in the light before Cornelius plunged it deep into Anzo's abdomen.

Anzo screamed just before he had his mouth covered by Cornelius.

"You will not ruin this. I'm sorry, but you will just interfere," said Cornelius, staring into Anzo's eyes.

Anzo struggled against him but it was futile. Anzo's strength was fleeting and Cornelius watched the light slowly leave his dark green eyes. Anzo slumped onto his knees, where Cornelius toppled him over. At that moment, Ryan rushed into the room.

"I heard someone yell, what happened?!" asked Ryan, slightly out of breath.

"I believe you heard me stub my toe against the island here. I'm quite clumsy in my old age," said Cornelius, panting but smiling slightly.

"Are you okay?" asked Ryan, inching closer.

"Stay there! I am fine, there is no need to worry, really," said Cornelius. He pushed the blade deep under the island's countertop. The blood was now dripping on the floor. Cornelius looked down and saw the pool of blood from Anzo making its way toward the sides of the island, clearly into Ryan's view. Cornelius was starting to sweat.

"So, is there anything else I can do for you?" said Cornelius.

"Um, no, I don't think so," said Ryan.

"Well, I should get back to it," said Cornelius, nodding toward the sink.

"Oh, yeah. Sure," said Ryan. "Goodnight."

"Goodnight," said Cornelius quickly.

Cornelius watched Ryan leave the room for a second time.

"Now, what am I going to do with you?" said Cornelius quietly to himself. Cornelius dragged Anzo to the porch and threw his body over the edge. "I'll bury you later. First I need to clean up."

He returned to the kitchen and grabbed a large towel and some bleach, he kneeled to begin cleaning up the blood.

After about an hour, Cornelius finally cleaned up all the blood, the towel was stained a dark red and Cornelius had to throw it in the trash.

Shame though, thought Cornelius. *I liked that towel.*

He sighed and glared out the glass doors, the beach was illuminated with moonlight.

"Damn. The body," said Cornelius, pushing his hands on his thighs to stand up. He opened a drawer and fumbled around for something.

"Ah, there you are," said Cornelius in a hushed voice. He pulled a long, black metal rod out of the drawer and closed the drawer silently.

Cornelius rushed to get out the door. He stepped outside and removed his vest, rolled up his sleeves, and walked down the stairs to Anzo's body. Cornelius dragged him underneath the porch. He felt around on the flashlight with his thumb before clicking it on. The flashlight buzzed to life, he shined the bright light on Anzo's abdomen where his shirt was stained with blood. He moved the light to Anzo's face, it was covered in sand and had a few insects crawling around. Cornelius watched in slight horror as one bug crawled into his mouth and another over his open eyes. Cornelius turned away, he sighed and walked further under the porch to a large plastic storage bin. From inside the bin, Cornelius grabbed a large metal shovel.

As he returned to Anzo's body, Cornelius sighed and placed the flashlight on the ground beside him and began shoveling sand. Cornelius dug until he could feel blisters on his hand starting to form. The hole was about waist deep before Cornelius climbed out and rolled Anzo's body in. Cornelius watched as each shovelful of sand slowly covered him, the sand hitting his chest and rolling down his sides and up his neck.

Once Cornelius had buried Anzo's body, he hid the shovel back inside the bin and walked out from under the porch. As he turned to go up the stairs to the house, he saw a flash of lightning over the ocean. Cornelius felt uneasy, there was a storm coming.

Once inside, Cornelius returned the flashlight to its drawer and headed back to his room. Cornelius was heading up the stairs and taking off his blazer when he realized that he had blood on his white dress shirt from where the blade had been kept. Cornelius threw his head back and sighed. He folded his blazer over his arm and covered up the blood stain as best he could. Upon arriving at his bedroom door, he reached into his back pocket and retrieved his key. After he unlocked his door, he threw the blazer on his bed and began to undress. Cornelius went into his bathroom and turned on the water in his shower.

Fortunately for him, his shower was offset far enough that the other tenants could not hear him. Cornelius placed both hands on the edge of the sink and stared at himself in the mirror. The steam from the shower began fogging up the mirror before Cornelius finally stepped into in the shower. The warm water soothed his muscles, it was a relief to clean himself of all the sweat and sand that came from burying Anzo. Whilst in the shower, Cornelius had the sudden realization that Anzo most likely didn't lock his own door, and that would lead to more questions.

"Why is nothing ever easy?" groaned Cornelius.

He turned off his shower and wrapped a robe around himself as he got out.

Cornelius snuck out of the room and headed to Anzo's room. He reached the door and grabbed the brass handle, turning it slowly. His muscles ached at the tension, but Cornelius was able to open it without a sound. He entered the room and closed the door behind him, just as painstakingly as when he entered. He looked around the inside and, like he had expected, the room was a mess and terribly disoriented. Cornelius scoffed and exited the room, he locked the door from the inside and decided to take the key from Anzo's body the next day, he was too tired to dig him up again tonight.

Cornelius sighed and returned to his room to get the dagger. Upon getting it, he returned to Anzo's door and with long, deep strokes, Cornelius began to scrape the name off the door.

Cornelius returned to his room and collapsed on his bed. He rolled over to one side and kissed a frayed, yellowed picture on the night desk next to his bed. The picture was of Cornelius and a lovely young woman with blonde hair.

I wish you were still here. Everything would be so different.

Better. Cornelius thought before he drifted off into a deep

sleep.

CHAPTER 13

Ryan rose the next morning to his nose running. He ran the backside of his hand underneath his nose to catch the dripping liquid but it did not stop running. Ryan looked down to find bright crimson blood was smeared across his hand. Ryan got up very quickly, but in doing so, he got lightheaded and grabbed his bed for balance. What was happening to him? He had been fine the previous day but now he suddenly felt very ill.

Ryan went to his bathroom and hung his head over his sink. He watched the droplets of blood drip and splatter over the white porcelain of the sink. It was oddly beautiful, the bright red staining the pure and perfect white of the sink. Ryan ran the tap and watched, mesmerized, as the blood drops swirled and danced in the bright sink. Coming out of his trance, he took some toilet tissue and pinched his nose shut. Once the bleeding subsided, Ryan couldn't find what he found so fascinating about the blood anymore. Ryan turned on the sink and washed the droplets away.

Ryan washed his hands and decided to head out to breakfast a little early. He hoped he could snag a cup of coffee before anyone noticed. With that thought in mind, Ryan's mood peaked a bit. He brushed his teeth and dressed himself before heading downstairs. As he made his way towards the steps, he saw another tenant, a blonde headed woman. She was tall and thin, her hair bounced with each step.

"Good morning, I don't think we've met, I'm Ryan," he said, extending out his hand. The woman continued walking and made her way down the steps without a second look. Ryan felt himself blush in embarrassment, and his mood was quickly soured. When Ryan made it down the stairs and turned the corner, he was greeted not by the joy of seeing the breakfast lie out and ready on the table, but instead an empty room. It seemed as though Cornelius didn't make breakfast. In fact, it didn't seem like Cornelius even entered the room. There was a faint smell of bleach in the air emitting from the kitchen and it quickly turned Ryan's stomach.

Instead, Ryan left the rooms to go out onto the porch, hoping the sea breeze would calm his stomach. Unfortunately for Ryan, as he stepped out unto the porch he noticed the the ocean was not calm, there were dark clouds swirling in the distance, a sure sign of an impending storm. Ryan felt a drop of rain pelt his nose. He looked down to see dark circles of rain appearing over the floorboards as the drops fell from the sky. There was something that didn't quite make sense. An extremely dark trio of droplets was a few feet from where Ryan was standing. Ryan bent down on one knee and placed his fingers into the mysterious liquid, but it was already dry, it looked like blood or some other dark stain.

This doesn't mean anything malicious happened here.

Someone could have stepped on a seashell or gotten a nosebleed like me.

I hope it's all a coincidence.

At that moment, a bolt of lightning danced in front of his eyes, followed by a faint thunderclap several seconds later. Ryan stood up and turned to face the door. When he saw Cornelius on the other side of the glass, Ryan gasped softly. Cornelius' expression was one of fear… and anger. He had a large scowl on his face and his forehead was scrunched into a tight ball.

Ryan felt uneasy. His stomach was not calmed from the breeze, and the finding of possible blood didn't help either. Ryan moved his fingers behind his butt. He reached up on the inside of the waistband of his jeans and wiped his fingers vigorously to remove the blood. Ryan began walking to the door when Cornelius disappeared. Ryan wondered if he had done something wrong.

Ryan opened the sliding door slowly and saw Cornelius hunched over the stove, cooking something. Ryan hesitated to shut the door, but he eventually did.

"I found some dark stains that looked like blood, should we look into it?" asked Ryan quietly

"I'm sure someone just stepped on a seashell, or had a nosebleed or something." replied Cornelius without turning around

Ryan's heart skipped a beat, Ryan found it odd that Cornelius would say the same exact thing he thought of.

"Don't you know there's a storm coming? It's dangerous for you to be out there, Ryan," Cornelius said monotonously. It seemed he didn't want to stay on the subject.

"Yeah, but it's pretty far away," said Ryan.

"You'd best be careful. Being reckless like that could put all of us in jeopardy," said Cornelius.

"If that's the case, we should leave the beach," replied Ryan sarcastically.

"Is this some kind of joke to you?" snarled Cornelius. He slapped the wooden spoon on the countertop next to him but still didn't face Ryan directly.

"What's a joke is you questioning me for opening a damn door. What is your problem?" fought Ryan.

"My problem is arrogant people like you. I took you in, I paid your bills, I feed you, and you go out and do something stupid like this!" Cornelius said raising his voice

"Are you kidding me? I went out for fresh air, and that's all." snapped Ryan. "Forget it. I'll just take some coffee and head to my room.".

He had said it, but in fact, he did not want to go near Cornelius. Ryan could tell Cornelius was angry, and Ryan wasn't sure what he would do to him. Ryan approached the cupboard and drew a ceramic mug from the shelf. He turned to pour himself a cup of coffee, all the while keeping a side eye on Cornelius. Cornelius didn't move an inch aside from stirring the pot. There was tension in his shoulders. Ryan grabbed his mug and left annoyed. This was not how he wanted to start his day. Cornelius looked over his shoulder and listened intently as Ryan walked out of the room.

Son of a bitch…. How much does he know?

Cornelius continued to stir a thick sauce in the pot in front of him. he lifted the spoon up and out of the pot. Cornelius' mind felt heavy. If Ryan found out about Anzo, things would end terribly. Cornelius took a deep breath and exhaled loudly. He didn't want to have to deal with Ryan the same way. Cornelius tasted he sauce and scowled at it, it was very bitter.

CHAPTER 14

Ryan headed up the stairs and toward his room. He took his key out of his pocket and began to place the key in the keyhole when he heard some sniffling. Ryan froze in place and turned his head slightly to see the woman that was with Anzo outside of his door. Ryan could barely remember her name. He was uninterested to learn it, however.

"You okay?" asked Ryan.

"What do you care? I bet you did this," snapped the woman.

"I'm not sure what you're talking about…" responded Ryan softly.

"Of course not, right? You're the innocent one. You're just a man trying to find his way back. Let me tell you something, this place isn't a home. It's a prison," sniffled the woman. "Maybe you should check out the library again, I'm sure you'll find all your answers there," spat the woman.

Ryan opened his mouth to respond but found it best to just stay quiet. Instead, Ryan sighed and turned back to his room. Ryan opened his door and placed his coffee mug on his nightstand. He sat down on his bed and went into deep thought.

Ryan knew that things were not as perfect as they seemed, but something bothered Ryan. In the back of his mind, he could feel that something dangerous and dark was looming over not only himself, but also the entire house. However, Ryan did have some trouble trusting these people when each person told him something different.

Tonight I'll go to the library and check it out. Let me see what else is there, and then if it's nothing, I'll just ignore her.

Ryan let out a short breath. As he closed his eyes, and could have sworn he heard a faint beeping noise. He felt nervous and scared already, this noise did not ease his tension. There was a sudden knock on Ryan's door. He jumped at the sound of it.

"H-hey, Ryan? It's Frank. Breakfast is ready," said Frank through the door.

"Jesus," said Ryan under his breath. He could feel his heartbeat in his throat. "Um, thanks Frank. I'll be out soon," said Ryan.

He could hear the footsteps of Frank retreating down the stairs.

Ryan had his plan, he just needed to enact it, and he hoped he would find nothing. But deep down, Ryan hoped there was something there.

Ryan went to breakfast and sat at the table, now there were two seats missing. Ryan kept his head down throughout the meal. Ryan glanced sideways to the other tenants, trying to piece together who was missing. The other tenants didn't notice or chose to ignore it. Ryan ate his food and drank his second cup of coffee. Once everyone was finished, Ryan caught Cornelius by the sink. He waited until the tenants left, he noticed the tan man and the other women, finally Frank made his way out.

"Hey Cornelius, let me ask you something," said Ryan placing his hands on the island countertop.

"Go ahead," replied Cornelius, he was visibly exhausted but continued to stack plates in the sink

"Have other tenants left? I noticed less and less people at the table," said Ryan softly.
The plates clattered in the sink, Cornelius looked up with tension in his shoulders.

"Yes. Some of the other tenants broke our agreement. I had to let them go unfortunately." Cornelius said bitterly.

"What'd they do?" Asked Ryan clenching his grip on the counter

"That's none of your concern," said Cornelius sternly, their eyes fixed on each other

Ryan felt a knot in his stomach tighten. Cornelius' tone made Ryan a little fearful.

"I think it-" Ryan was soon cut off.

"Hey guys, e-e-everything alright?" Stuttered Frank

"Everything's fine Frank, thank you," said Cornelius dully, turning to resume his cleaning. There was fear in Frank's eyes, Ryan let his grip of the counter go,

"Frank, can I talk to you for a second?" said Ryan, fixating on Cornelius' back.

"S-sure," responded Frank

The pair left the room and Cornelius resumed his cleaning.

Before Ryan could get out a word, Frank gripped Ryan's arm. Ryan felt his scar flare up and burn.

"You need to stop," said Frank sternly.

"Why? What do you know?" demanded Ryan as he pulled it away from Frank.

"You're bordering on dangerous territory Ryan. Stay clear of it." said frank softly. He turned and began walking up the stairs. Ryan waited for a minute but eventually followed suit, he had to wait until nightfall.

CHAPTER 15

Ryan sat on his bed and watched the sun creep away, the light slowly fading, turning his room all shades of colors from orange and red to purple and blue. The colors still reminded him of his childhood out on the hammock. The thought relaxed Ryan for a moment, but soon, his reality set in once more. Ryan felt his stomach pinch, he was worried what he would find.

Ryan grabbed his journal gifted to him from Cornelius as well as the exquisite pen, he wrote in his journal: *Two people missing from the table today. Frank has been acting strange, going to the library tonight in search of answers. Wish me luck.*

Ryan twisted the pen closed and shut the journal. tapping the pen on the journal before putting it away. Ryan exited the room, and as he headed for the stairs, he had an encounter with another woman.

"Where are you heading so late?" breathed the woman.

She sniffled, and Ryan noticed she had been crying. Ryan wasn't sure how to respond to the woman. He opened his mouth but shut it again.

"who are you?" asked Ryan nervously, what would she tell Cornelius?

"I'm Daniella, but don't worry I'm sure you won't see me much after this." she said coldly.

"Can I ask why?" said Ryan, trying to remain calm.

"I'm leaving this place. I mean, haven't you figured it out? It's not safe here," she said crossing her arms and leaning against the doorway.

"Yeah," sighed Ryan, still on edge.

Ryan smirked at the woman and turned to leave again. Ryan could feel the woman's eyes follow him, and as Ryan reached the stairway, he hesitated. He turned to face the woman again.

"Would you by any chance happen to know of any pictures of all tenants or something similar?" inquired Ryan. He wanted to be as subtle about his question as possible.

"Yeah, in the library there's a photobook somewhere. It's really big and it's usually on a table, not on the shelf.," responded the woman. She sniffled and retreated into her room. Ryan nodded and continued down the steps to the library.

A muffled boom of thunder cracked, distracting Ryan from his thoughts. Ryan breathed deeply but his thoughts persisted. Ryan needed to find out who was missing and why. Ryan was giddy from excitement. It was fun to play a detective.

CHAPTER 16

Sitting on his bed, Cornelius twirled a heavy metal key in his hands, it was red on one side from blood. Cornelius was on edge, he felt highly suspicious of Ryan.

If he ever found out about…. No, he can't. There's no evidence.

Cornelius left his room and headed towards Anzo's bedroom, as he stood in front of the door, he murmured.

"Sorry about this, old chap," he slid the key into the lock and slowly turned until the cylinders clicked and unlocked the door. Cornelius opened the door and disappeared inside.

Ryan walked around the library. He hoped he could find something in the photo book Daniella mentioned. He walked slowly in a large circle around the library, searching the bookshelf and fireplace mantle, but he did not find anything. Ryan's hope was diminishing but he persisted on finding it. He began moving in between the couches and the recliners. Behind the recliners, Ryan found a corner of a very large book poking out from under the worn leather of one of the recliners. Ryan looked around before bending down to retrieve it.

The book was old and frayed, but it followed the same black cover style as the others. Ryan cracked it open and the pages crinkled as they were spread, it was a pleasant sound to Ryan. He opened the book to the first page, it was a yellow and faded picture of what Ryan assumed was a young Cornelius in front of the house. It looked newly built. Ryan grinned at the sight of a full, dark haired Cornelius with a lack of wrinkles. Ryan continued through the pictures, nothing of significance stood out to him, there were several photos of people Ryan did not recognize as well as photos of Cornelius shaking hands with someone. Ryan continued flipping the pictures before he found something that peaked his interest. The photo was large, Ryan recognized many of the faces this time but not all. The photo was of the current tenants, with an aged Cornelius in the middle, he had a large smile on his face, he had his arm around someone who looked strangely familiar to Hannah…Ryan squinted to make out more details but it was unmistakable. Ryan also found Daniella, Greg, Frank in the back trying to hide from it, and Anzo off to the side with his arms crossed. Ryan counted each of the people and without a doubt there were two more people in the photo than Ryan remembered seeing at the table. Speaking of which, Anzo was the one who was missing from breakfast…Ryan continued to flip through the pages but the rest were all blank, he assumed he reached the end of the book.

Ryan returned the book underneath the recliner as best he could remember it, he had a direction, now how could he find out where Anzo went? *If he left willingly*, thought Ryan. Ryan left the library pondering how to get into Anzo's room, then it hit Ryan, maybe he could play dumb and just knock. Ryan nearly palmed his forehead, it was almost too simple. Ryan walked towards Anzo's room, his heart beat a little faster and his hands ran cold, but Ryan raised his hand and used the knuckle of one of his fingers to knock gently in the door. There was a moment of hesitation that left Ryan breathless, but there was no answer. Ryan reached up again and just before he could make contact with the door, it opened to Ryan's surprise. Ryan could not hide his shocked expression,

"Hi Cornelius," said Ryan as calm as he could.

"Ryan. Is there something you need?" Replied Cornelius ignoring Ryan's shock.

"What are you doing here? Where's Anzo?" asked Ryan while trying to peer into the room, Ryan didn't see anything out of place except the drapes blowing in the wind.

"Anzo has left the estate. It was not to his liking, I am cleaning his room now, so if you don't mind, I should get back to it." Cornelius slammed the door before Ryan could even respond.

Cleaning it or cleaning it out? thought Ryan. *Strange that the window was open, it's probably freezing out.*

Ryan pondered to himself before he decided to head outside, he could sneak out the sliding door and try to find a ladder or something to peer into Anzo's room.

As Ryan exited the house, the chill from the ocean breeze gave Ryan goose bumps, and he rubbed his arms to try and keep warm. He walked off the porch and around the house. The sand was freezing, it was practically snow. As Ryan walked, nothing stood out to him. It looked like a normal beach house. Ryan was beginning to get frustrated by the lack of conviction. Everything was too perfect. Ryan groaned loudly, but he was muted by a louder noise. Something crashed to the ground. It sounded like it originated from around the corner on the back edge where the bedroom windows were.

Yes! Finally!

Ryan's adrenaline was pumping again, as he felt his hands go cold and numb. He ran towards the sound, but stopped at the corner to peak from a distance. In the dark, it was hard to see exactly what had happened. Ryan waited for something, anything to move in the dark. There was nothing for a while, but the clouds began shifting and the moonlight began to shine through in streaks.

Ryan could now see parts of the ground. There was a small dresser half in the sand, and there were several books and pens scattered around the impact area. Ryan looked up and saw the window wide open. As Ryan looked up, more items began flying out of the window as if of their own volition.

Ryan continued waiting to see what else would happen. To his dismay, nothing else happened. Ryan could see the items easily in the moonlight, but nothing caught his attention. Ryan sifted through the junk and found only some old raunchy magazines and newspaper clippings.

Ryan was about to give up his search through the items when a gleam of moonlight shone off a corner of something mostly buried in the sand. Ryan dug the sand out from around the object and discovered a journal. A black leather journal that was similar to Ryan's, it had the initials AS engraved in it. Ryan ran his fingers along the middle of the book to untie the string when he heard some shuffling from the open window. Ryan stuck half of the book in his waistband behind his back, he covered the other half with his jacket.

Ryan decided to sneak back into the house through the kitchen sliding door. Unfortunately for Ryan, the door was locked. Ryan had to enter at the main entrance, but he didn't care. Ryan's curiosity was piqued. A delicious secret was hiding between the walls of this mansion.

Ryan entered the mansion to one dimmed light in the hall. It was very dark through the house. Ryan locked the door behind him and made his way up the stairs as quietly as he could. Ryan went to the door of his room and saw a light breaking the silence of the darkness coming from underneath the door of Cornelius's bedroom.

Ryan unlocked his door and entered it. He took off his shoes and out came an abundance of sand. Ryan didn't expect anything else, honestly. He took off his socks and rolled his jeans up to his mid-shin. He removed the journal from behind his back and began untying the knot from the small leather straps.

A thick silence engulfed Ryan's room. His ears were clogged with the silence and he could hear his own blood rushing through. The static in his ears caused his heart to beat faster.

As the knot was undone, the journal cracked open, but it had no smell. The pages were slightly torn and in bad shape, Anzo didn't care for it it seemed. Ryan flipped through all the pages, most of them were blank aside from the occasional rant about a "new tenant," which Ryan only guessed was about him. Ryan reached the end of the book but noticed there were some pages torn out forcefully, they left large pieces behind, it looked rushed. Ryan turned the book over and shook it to try and find any lingering pages that were stuck, but nothing came out. Ryan tossed the book onto his bed in defeat, it was another dead end. Ryan placed the journal under his mattress, hopefully it was well hidden enough. Ryan laid on his bed until his eyes couldn't stay open anymore. He soon drifted to sleep.

Ryan woke up in his bed in the middle of the night to the sound of faint beeping. Ryan sat upright to listen carefully, the beeps were consistent, like the hospital machines. Ryan closed his eyes to try and listen intently for it, he could have sworn he also heard faint talking, but it sounded like Ryan was hearing it from underwater. The noises eventually disappeared, and there was nothing but silence in the room. Maybe the stress of the information he'd found was taking its toll on him. Ryan stood up and turned on a small lamp by his bedside table. He rubbed his face with his palms. Ryan had a bad taste in his mouth he needed to wash out, but didn't want to go down the stairs, and instead, he got up and walked to his bathroom. Ryan flicked the light on, and the bright light seared into his head and made his eyes ache. He could barely keep them open.

Ryan made his way to the sink while keeping his eyes closed. He turned on the faucet and held his hands cupped under the spout. Nothing had come out. Ryan opened his right eye and could see no water was running. Ryan waited until his eyes adjusted and fully opened them. His head ached from the light. Ryan turned the faucet handles all the way open, but nothing came out. He bent down under the sink and checked for any leaks. He didn't see anything out of the ordinary.

Ryan sighed and stood up straight again. He put his hands on the edges of the sink and stared into the sink. Ryan slowly lifted his head, and from the corner of the sink, he could see the bathtub. Ryan turned to face the tub and saw red vein-like vines sprouting from the faucet. They came out of the faucet and wrapped around the spout.

"What the hell?" said Ryan under his breath.

Ryan reached out and touched the vines. They were warm and thumped like a distant heartbeat. Maybe he could flush out whatever was inside?

Ryan reached around the spout and turned the faucet handles. The pipes groaned behind the tiled wall and reverberated off the spout. Ryan watched in anticipation, and just before he gave up on it, a slow drip began. Ryan crouched and got his face closer to the spout.

In that moment black sludge began pouring out forcefully. It was thick and came out in a large spurt. Ryan closed the faucet as quick as he could, but it had no effect. The liquid kept pouring out and did not seem to have an end in sight.

"Shit!" said Ryan fearfully.

Soon after, though, the sludge stopped of its own volition. Ryan realized he was breathing heavily and sweating. Ryan grabbed the edge of the tub and peered in. Ryan could not see the bottom of the tub. The inky black liquid pooled and devoured all the light that hit it. It sat flat like asphalt, and if Ryan hadn't seen it pour out, he could guarantee that it was completely solid. Ryan reached over the edge and dipped two of his fingers into the liquid. It was freezing cold. He rubbed the sludge between his thumb and two fingers. It was very thick and had no smell, but it gave Ryan a sense of dread.

Ryan released a short breath through his nose. He grabbed the edge of the bathtub to lift himself off the ground when a black hand reached out from the substance and grabbed his wrist. Ryan yelped as the frigid cold pierced his skin down to his bones. Ryan tried to pull his wrist away, but the hand was too strong. Ryan slipped off the edge, and his hand was pulled into the dark pool.

His arm should have hit the bottom, but it felt endless. His arm kept going deeper into the pit, the sludge swallowing every inch. He soon lost feeling in his hand and arm. The pit was arctic, and Ryan began to panic. He began breathing heavily, and his heart was beating hard. Ryan tried to struggle against the pool, but it was overwhelmingly powerful. If Ryan pulled any harder, he would surely dislocate his shoulder.

A dark face began to emerge from the substance. It was somewhat humanlike, but it had no features, like a drawing of a man that was smeared and twisted. It began rising, coming face to face with Ryan. It appeared to open its mouth to speak, but it sounded like nails on a chalkboard. Ryan winced at the sound. His distraction was his doom as the other hand of the monster reached up and grabbed Ryan's opposite shoulder.

Ryan could barely resist the monster. It slowly returned into the depths of the black pool pulling Ryan with it. It was too late. The cold was setting in and Ryan began shaking violently and was losing strength. He could see his breath as his face got closer to the pool. There was a moment of hesitation. The beast released his grip slightly, and Ryan used this moment to try and escape, but it was futile. The monster let out one more shriek from below the surface of the sludge. It echoed as if the pool was a cave.

Ryan heard a voice in the distance…"Ryyyaannnn." It reverberated off the walls and Ryan began panicking.

Ryan whimpered, and the monster pulled Ryan's head under the surface. Ryan could not see anything in the darkness. Ryan struggled, but the sludge was too thick. It filled his ears, nose, and mouth. It slowly slid down his throat cutting off his breathing and the sludge slid into his lungs, pushing the remaining air out. Ryan's heart began to slow as the voice repeated "let go...let go"

Ryan awoke in a cold sweat, his shirt clung to him as he began kicking his covers off. He sat up and looked down at his hands and watched his fingers shake, he held his hands close to his chest to calm them. He looked around the room, but it was quiet. *Was it just another nightmare?*

Ryan stood and made his way to the bathroom, he flicked the light switch on and his heart skipped a beat. The light burned his eyes but they quickly adjusted, there was no sign of the black sludge. He tried to control his breathing and calm down. Ryan thought it was unexpected as he never usually had nightmares, but they were happening almost everyday now.

Ryan turned the faucet and watched the water overflow in his hands, losing himself in his thoughts. His life went from being perfectly normal to being turned completely upside down. He lost the only thing in his life that was worth living for. Ryan raised his cupped hands to his face, and the splash of ice cold water soothed him, Ryan repeated the process a few more times before he turned the water off and stared at himself in the mirror. The water dripping off his face and his hair tousled in all directions. His eyes looked different, he felt different. He *was* different.

Ryan grabbed the towel hanging nearby and dried his face. He exited the bathroom and decided to make his way downstairs. Ryan headed into the kitchen as he heard the wind blowing outside, the storm was getting closer. Ryan grabbed a glass out of the cupboard and poured himself a glass of apple juice, Ryan was surprised at how sweet it was. This apple juice was delicious and it brought back memories of his childhood. Ryan downed the glass and placed the glass in the sink. Ryan turned to leave the room but something on the floor caught his eye. Ryan crouched to take a better look. It was a small dark dot, though it didn't look like a knot in the wood, so he laid his finger on it. It was dry. He couldn't tell what it was, but Ryan assumed it was nothing and stood up. He went around the island to walk out of the kitchen when he spotted another dot. This one was smaller in size. If the hardwood was not so light in color, he would have never spotted it.

Ryan continued to follow the dots but was stumped when the trail dropped off. Ryan looked up and stared at his reflection in the glass of the sliding door. Cornelius really did keep this place spotless. Ryan got closer to the sliding door and stared off into the horizon. From the porch stairs you could still see the ocean. The moon illuminated the waves and the sand glistened like fresh snow on a winter morning. Ryan sighed and lost himself while staring out. It was peaceful and calming. Ryan could feel his urge to sleep creep up and pull him back. Ryan turned around and returned to his room. Once there, he opened his bedroom window and let the sound of the waves of the ocean rock him to sleep.

Ryan slept through the night with no more interruptions and no more dreams. He rose up slightly earlier this morning and decided to go for a walk on the beach. The sand was very inviting, and he craved feeling the sand between his toes. Ryan got up and took off his pajamas. He looked down at his body and could see the scars from the crash on his arm and leg.

Ryan traced the outline of the scar with his hand. He saw visions of the crash flash before his eyes. As he closed his eyes tightly, his hand trembled. He tried to push it out of his mind. Ryan was cold, he found a flannel shirt that belonged to his father. Ryan was surprised to see it, he didn't remember packing it. Ryan took it when his father had left it after Ryan's mom passed. Wearing it now felt like home. Leaving his shoes behind, Ryan walked down the stairs as quietly as he could.

Ryan went into the kitchen, hoping to sneak a cup of coffee before his walk. He was shocked to see Cornelius standing in the kitchen, facing the window over the sink.

"Good morning," said Cornelius quietly. He looked like he hasn't slept in days.

"Good morning…. You okay?" asked Ryan.

"Yeah, just old age getting to me," responded Cornelius with a smirk.

"Gotcha. Well, I was just going to grab a cup of coffee and go for a walk on the beach, if you want to join me," said Ryan reluctantly. He didn't want to make Cornelius feel left out, but he was hoping Cornelius didn't want to join him.

Cornelius turned and looked at Ryan for a while. He raised his hand to a patch of hair that was sticking up and pressed it down. He turned his gaze down toward the floor.

"That's very generous, but no, thank you. I have quite a bit of work to do around the house today. Maybe next time," said Cornelius.

"Alright," responded Ryan gently.

Ryan grabbed a mug out of the cabinet and filled it with the dark elixir of caffeine. He dropped in some sugar and watched it sink to the bottom. A vision of the dark figure from his nightmare burned into his mind. Ryan shook it off, he had no time to waste remembering that nightmare.

Ryan poured in some milk. He watched as the white milk danced and folded over and under with the dark coffee, embracing each other but never fully being intertwined. Ryan caught himself getting lost in it, but the sun was just beginning to rise. Ryan plunged his spoon into the drink and stirred vigorously before exiting out the sliding door.

The wood felt damp against Ryan's feet from the morning dew. Ryan took a sip of his coffee and groaned audibly. The bitter liquid felt like heaven in his mouth. It was delicious. Ryan walked down the steps. Once in the sand, Ryan dug his toes in. The sand was frigid, causing Ryan's skin to rise with goose bumps again. As the sun rose, the ocean glinted like a piece of fine jewelry-the ocean breeze gently wafted through the air.

Peace washed over Ryan. Out of all his days here, this morning was just excellent, away from everyone. Ryan walked down to the coastline, sipping his coffee as he went. As Ryan continued on, he took notice of the dark clouds off in the distance. Like a dark wall, they gave Ryan a sense of dread. Ryan walked for a few more minutes along the shore but decided to head back to avoid being late for breakfast.

On the way back toward the house, Ryan moved closer to the water, having the waves wash over his feet. It was a remarkable feeling. Ryan's feet were cold from the sand, but the ocean felt slightly warmer---or maybe it was his imagination. Ryan's feet submerged as the white foam crashed over them. He looked out into the distance across the sand and saw a family of three sitting in lawn chairs under an umbrella. Ryan hadn't realized there were other people nearby. Ryan squinted to see: he made out a little boy who was building a sand castle as his mother helped, and a father who sat in a lawn chair, seemingly disappointed to be with them. It felt as if Ryan was peering at his own childhood. Ryan continued walking, but as he got closer, the image disappeared. Ryan supposed it was inevitable, the beach always brought memories back to him, both good and bad. Ryan shook his head and turned his gaze to the house now right next to him.

Ryan didn't want to return just yet. Something about being in the house set his teeth on edge. Something wasn't right. Recently, Ryan felt a different vibe from the tenants and especially Cornelius. When Ryan first met Cornelius, he was very well kept, with gelled hair and a clean pressed suit. But as each day passed, his hair became a little messier, his suit just slightly more wrinkled and crimped. Ryan also noticed that Cornelius was also on edge. He seemed very paranoid, like he was hiding something.

Ryan finished his last sip and stared over the ocean. The wind picked up and blew through his hair. Ryan took a deep breath and shut his eyes for a moment. Ryan released his breath and began to walk back inside. It was the first nice day in a while, but he didn't want to waste it. Alas, he had to return for breakfast.

As Ryan began walking back to the stairs, he got a whiff of something putrid. Ryan had to keep himself from gagging. His eyes were watery, but Ryan had no idea what was causing this horrid smell.

Ryan began searching around but could only see the ocean of golden sand around him. He began to run towards the stairs when Ryan's heart dropped. What he saw shook him to his core, and his stomach tensed up into a knot. He felt like vomiting and screaming at the same time. Ryan dropped his mug into the sand and continued to stare in horror.

Through the steps, Ryan saw an extremely pale hand sticking straight out of the ground from the sand. The hand was obviously human, but it was twisted and rotting, like it could have never belonged to a living person. The smell coming from it was unimaginable. The smell of rotting flesh and decay. It was enough to make Ryan feel light headed.

Ryan gasped, but breathing in the stench was making him sick. He grabbed his cup from the sand and ran up the stairs, tripping as he did. He ran toward the door and slid it open violently.

Cornelius faced the sink but was visibly startled when Ryan opened the door. Ryan was struggling to get any words out. He couldn't tell anyone what he saw. Either they wouldn't believe him, or they would think he did it. Ryan was gasping for air when Cornelius began questioning him.

"Are you alright? What happened?" asked Cornelius.

"Um…I was walking along the bank and something touched my foot," replied Ryan pointing with his thumb over his shoulder. He couldn't control his horror, he hoped Cornelius hadn't noticed. Ryan only hoped that Cornelius would buy it.

Cornelius looked at Ryan for a second with a concerned and confused look on his face.

"Sure.... Okay, well, give me your mug. I'll wash it," said Cornelius calmly.

"Thanks," said Ryan. He raised the mug to give it to Cornelius, but he realized he was trembling. Ryan placed the mug on the counter and slid it over to Cornelius. "I think I'm going to go wash my foot," said Ryan monotonously. Ryan rushed out of the kitchen and ran up to his room, slamming his door behind him

Ryan leaned against the back of his door and slid to the ground. He put his hands into his hair and waited breathlessly, his mind was moving so quick it felt like it was standing still.

Was that a dead body? Was that a tenant or...someone else?

Ryan's stomach tensed up, but this time, he couldn't hold it in. Ryan ran into his bathroom and vomited in his toilet. Ryan slowly stood up and went to the sink to wash his mouth out. The cool water made him feel slightly better, but the knot in his stomach remained. Ryan slumped down next to the toilet and groaned. What was he going to do? Someone was obviously dead but he didn't know who it was or why it happened. He had many questions and yet Ryan felt none of them could be answered, unless someone in the house knew about it.

Ryan sat for a while before he decided he should get down to breakfast. Ryan pushed himself up using the toilet edge. Ryan looked at himself in the mirror and tried pushing his hair out of the way to make it seem like nothing had happened.

Downstairs Ryan could smell Cornelius was preparing breakfast like any day, but he was weary of the encounter between the two of them. *Was I too nervous? I hope he doesn't think anything of it.* Ryan thanked Cornelius for the meal and returned to his room as quickly as he could. Ryan's mind was far from this house, somewhere distant where no one could join him

CHAPTER 17

Cornelius, on the other hand, was very suspicious of Ryan, he hadn't seen him so shaken before. Nothing could have washed ashore to "touch his foot" and there certainly wasn't anything on the beach….except…

Could he have found him? thought Cornelius. *Damn him! He ruined everything. I need to fix this…but it's too early. Someone could see me.*

Cornelius pondered what to do. He raised his hand to his forehead and began rubbing the skin in circles.

"Everything okay, C-c-Cornelius?" stuttered Frank.

"Yes. Everything is fine now," whispered Cornelius. He stopped rubbing his head and used his hand to mask his smile.

"Frank, I need your help with something. Don't tell anyone and meet me outside on the beach side porch in five minutes," said Cornelius sternly, moving all the plates around in the sink to make it seem like he was busy.

"S-s-s-sure thing, Cornelius. I'll be there," replied Frank.

Cornelius shuffled some dirty plates from breakfast around. He watched Frank leave out of the corner of his eye. He dried his hands and went to the cabinet. He grabbed one of the large chef knives and glanced at it. He twirled it in his hand and placed a finger to the tip. A tiny droplet of blood leaked out. He dried it on the towel once more.

You don't deserve my other knife. That's reserved for special people.

He carefully placed the knife on the inside of his blazer, pressing against his chest. He held it with his left hand and pulled the jacket over with his right hand

Cornelius continued to step out onto the patio, still clutching the knife silently. He found Frank standing with his back turned. He took the knife out, but instead pulled it around to his back, out of view. Cornelius grabbed Frank firmly with his right hand.

"Ready?" said Cornelius slyly with a smile.

"I think s-s-so," responded Frank weakly.

Cornelius nodded and smiled once more. He gestured toward the stairs and said, "We're going to be doing some work under the stairs today."

Frank slowly made his way to the stairs. Cornelius followed in short pursuit. Once they reached the bottom of the stairs, a horrible stench crept over them. It was inevitable. The grave Cornelius had dug for Anzo was too shallow, and Cornelius knew it. There was just never enough time in a day to get everything he wanted done. Cornelius pulled a handkerchief from his pocket and covered his nose and mouth.

"Must have been a wild animal or something," mumbled Cornelius.

"Cornelius, w-w-what is that?!" whimpered Frank as he pointed to an exposed hand, pale as moonlight sticking out of the sand.

Cornelius pulled the knife from his back and held it to Frank's throat. He pushed the tip through the skin and watched the blood dribble out in a small stream.

"Listen to me. If you so much as scream, I will cut your throat so quickly you won't even realize you're bleeding," said Cornelius in a hushed voice. "You're going to dig up this body, and you will dig a new grave. You will bury it so deep, no one will ever know about this. You understand me?"

"Yes-s-s, sir," replied Frank, barely audible.

Cornelius pulled the knife from Frank's throat. Frank clutched his skin and saw he was bleeding. Cornelius glared at Frank, his eyes piercing through him. Cornelius pointed with the knife to the side where a shovel was leaning nearby, and Frank quickly picked up the shovel.

He gripped it tightly as he dug it into the ground.

CHAPTER 18

Ryan tried to get his senses back to normal. His head hurt from the constant questioning, the hand clawing its way through his mind. If he brought it up, it could be suspicious. If he didn't, then he could be blamed. Either way, the outcome would be bleak and dark.

Ryan sat on the edge of his bed and pondered the possibilities of what he could do. All of them ended in the same result. Nothing would be resolved, and Ryan would be asked questions he couldn't answer. Instead, Ryan came up with part of a solution: he would have to find out who was buried and who would want to kill them.

Ryan exited his room and went toward the library. As Ryan passed through the kitchen, he noticed the dishes weren't done. Cornelius usually would have cleaned them and packed them away about fifteen minutes after breakfast had passed, but it was almost noon, three hours since they had sat down for breakfast.

Ryan felt a knot in his stomach that something wasn't right. He continued to walk to the library, hoping he would find someone to talk to, but the rooms of the house were surprisingly vacant. No one in sight, Ryan continued to walk through the halls. His plan to solve this mystery was pushed to the back of his mind. This was far more pressing.

Ryan searched almost all the rooms but could not find anyone. He returned to the main hallway and there was an anomalous sensation in the air. Ryan felt as if he was being watched, as if somehow the tenants staring at him through the walls, watching his every move and breath. He became exceedingly uncomfortable. He began to walk toward the steps and heard a door close. Ryan held his breath to hear any movement at all but was met with silence. Ryan rushed up the steps and went to the first door he found. He knocked and waited patiently for anything to happen or to see any sign of moment or noise. Ryan's ears rang in anticipation, yearning to catch some hint of noise.

Ryan moved to the next door, and the next, but each one was met with the same end. Silence. Not even a whisper of a sound, not a murmur or bang. It was dead silent. In his entire time here, Ryan had never seen the halls this empty. Something didn't sit well with him. He knew something was happening, he just needed to figure out what.

Feeling slightly defeated, Ryan began to retreat to his room. There was no use if no one was willing to talk. He knew they were in there. There was nowhere else to go.

Ryan entered his room and just then remembered he hadn't actually gotten anything done. He was so preoccupied with trying to figure out where everyone was that he forgot to get supplies for his venture tonight. It seemed as though that would have to wait until after lunch.

CHAPTER 19

Cornelius looked at his watch and saw he was running out of time. He needed to wash the dishes and start preparing lunch. People would start to question if he wasn't around, but the new grave Frank was digging was barely finished. It could barely hold a body, so Cornelius decided on his next move.

"It doesn't look as though you'll be getting this done at the moment. I think you should go to your room and wash up, prepare for lunch," said Cornelius.

Frank was silent. He placed the shovel next to the uncompleted grave and slowly walked past Cornelius. Cornelius took this opportunity to grab Frank's arm. His grip was tight, enough to make Frank wince and whimper. Frank tried to claw off Cornelius's hand, but it was no use. Cornelius was too strong.

"Remember. No one can know about this," Cornelius said in a deep, hushed voice.

"Yes," responded Frank quickly.

Cornelius let go of Frank's arm, leaving a white mark where his fingers were. The white mark slowly turned pink and then red. Frank covered the spot with one hand and ran back up the stairs toward the house.

Cornelius continued to stay for a few seconds before beginning to leave. Before he went up the steps, however, he placed the knife under the very last step and covered it lightly with sand. He couldn't be taking knives all around the house with him.

Cornelius returned up the steps and entered the house. Frank was nowhere in sight.

CHAPTER 20

As one of the bedroom doors closed, Ryan's ears sprang to life, finally sensing what they were waiting for: a sound. Ryan heard the door close and jumped off his bed. He ran to his door and opened it but did not step out. Instead, he had stuck his head out to see if he could see the source of the noise without startling them, but again everything fell silent.

Damn! I almost had them. Ryan slowly slunk his head back behind the door frame, he felt beaten but he wasn't giving up. Ryan kept his ears honed for any slight movement. It was his only benefit being the third to last door and having only Cornelius next to him. There was not a single motion; not a stir, not a sound.

Ryan groaned and finally shut the door behind him. He placed his forehead on the wooden door and thought quietly to himself. There had to be a way to get people to talk to him. Ryan then had an idea. As the time for lunch began to creep closer, Ryan would sit at the bottom of the stairs and wait for everyone to come out of their rooms. That was his last chance to get any answers at all as to why they were being so elusive.

Ryan paced around his room and pondered whether his plan would work. Lunch was soon. Should he actually wait at the bottom of the stairs, or should he stay close to the door to the kitchen? Ryan didn't have much time to figure it out.

Ryan left the room and decided to stay close to the base of the staircase. He stood next to one of the decorative pillars. He waited for a while, and to his dismay, no one showed up. Ryan remained suspicious. They had to show up. Eventually.

Ryan waited five more minutes, but he too was going to be late and he wasn't sure what Cornelius would do. Ryan walked to the dining room and found all of the tenants sat at the table neatly, staring quietly up at Ryan. Ryan's jaw dropped. How was it possible they could have arrived before him? No one even passed by him.

"Better close your mouth. You might catch some flies standing like that," said Cornelius, looking smug. "I'll give you a warning this time. But next time you won't be so lucky. Don't be late again." Cornelius spoke sternly, as if all his joy had left.

Cornelius sat quietly and stared at Ryan before gesturing with his hand for Ryan to take a seat. Ryan moved quietly but swiftly. He could not comprehend what had just happened. He took his seat as fast as he could, and it was only in this moment that he realized, he wasn't hungry at all. He moved subconsciously, being controlled by something invisible. He ate even though he wasn't hungry and he drank when he wasn't thirsty.

The other tenants hadn't said a word. They all droned on and ate their lunch without a whisper. Ryan could have sworn they weren't even breathing by how quiet they were. For the first time, Ryan felt like he didn't belong. Not because he was new or different, but instead he felt like a defect machine, one capable of self-awareness when all the others were programmed to do what they do.

Lunch proceeded to end quickly and all the tenants stood at the same time, with the exception of Ryan of course. They all seemed to scatter like bees from a beehive. Each had a job to do, each their own goals to accomplish before the day was over. Ryan didn't question it. He had wanted everyone to leave. It was time to set his plan in motion and find out where that hand had come from.

Ryan could feel Cornelius's gaze studying him, but it didn't bother him. Ryan needed to do what he had to until it was finished. Once the table was cleared, Ryan made his way back toward his room. He saw Frank standing idly by the kitchen but said nothing to him. Instead, Ryan retreated to his room.

CHAPTER 21

Frank began shaking again. Cornelius kept watching his every move. Frank looked up to meet Cornelius' eyes. He could feel Cornelius's piercing gaze. Every time they made eye contact, Frank froze in place, only after breaking the contact did Frank continue to dig.

Frank quickly became uncomfortable and was walking out when he felt a tug on the back of his shirt. Frank stopped dead in his tracks, his sweat beading and sliding down his skin. There was a quick pull in which Frank yelped at the fear of falling. He felt a tug on his shirt, and he lost his balance and collapsed into Cornelius. Cornelius pulled Frank's head close to his so that his ear was near Cornelius` mouth.

"If you say anything to anyone about what happened here, it will be the last thing you do," spat Cornelius.

Frank shook with fear but nodded his head slowly, showing his understanding of what was said. Cornelius shoved Frank back onto his feet and pushed him away.

Cornelius dusted off his blazer and sighed deeply. Nothing was going according to plan and this was infuriating him. Cornelius continued to work on the dishes until nothing but steel sink remained. Cornelius could feel his eyes get heavy. He decided it was time to go to bed. He left the kitchen and began up the stairs. Most of the bedroom lights were off, except for Ryan's.

What could he possibly be doing in there?

But Cornelius was too tired to focus much on it. Instead, he continued toward his bedroom. He stripped himself of his clothes and changed into his pajamas. He picked up the picture on his bedside table. He then kissed his fingers and lovingly pressed them onto the frame. It was cold. Cornelius sighed once more and settled into his bed for what felt like a few minutes. Soon he was awoken by the light of the morning sun. Cornelius breathed deeply and willed himself out of bed to begin a new day once again.

CHAPTER 22

Ryan could hear shuffling from next door. He couldn't sleep at all, the vision of the white hand seared into his brain. Was it just his imagination? Could he possibly have thought of something so gruesome?

Or was it real?

Ryan gulped and looked at his own hands. They were nothing like what he saw. His hands were full of life, full of color. Ryan turned his gaze toward the door and decided he would inspect the makeshift grave as early as he could, not to be seen by anyone.

Ryan remembered that past the library was another sliding door that led to the beach. He could exit that way and find his way to the kitchen side door. It was Ryan's best chance at solving the mystery.

Ryan stood and moved toward the bathroom. Inside, he opened the medicine cabinet behind his mirror.

He grabbed a bottle and popped two of the bright purple pills into his mouth. Since last night, his head had been throbbing with a non-stop white hot pain. Ryan closed the cabinet door and looked at himself. Behind him, he could see the colorless eyes of Hannah from his nightmare. Ryan gasped and turned as fast as his body would let him, but there was nothing in the room. Ryan was breathing heavily before turning toward the mirror again.

In the mirror, the eyes looked back at him, their icy stare reflected back into Ryan's. He was frozen in shock. His once lively hands turned cold and white, almost deathly white. Ryan's breathing turned into a staggered gasp for air, as if he was being choked and denied any. The face tilted its head and opened its mouth. Its broken yellowed teeth appearing from behind its lips. It whispered something, but before it could reach Ryan's ears, a knock came from the door.

Ryan snapped out of his daze. He turned toward the door and tried to stutter words, but nothing would come out. Ryan returned his view toward the mirror but only saw himself staring back. His nervous eyes scanned all the corners of the mirror but there was no sign of her. Ryan could feel his cold sweat drip down the sides of his head. Ryan swallowed hard and moved his shaking feet towards the door.

Upon opening it however, there was no one at the door. Ryan was puzzled. He was sure he had heard a knock, but the hallway was empty. Ryan closed the door and stood in front of it for some time, waiting for something to happen, but nothing did. There was a thick stillness that held Ryan in place. Ryan gave up and headed out into the hallway.

It seemed to be pretty early in the morning. The sun shone through the tall windows onto the stairway. Ryan walked down and felt the warm spots where the sun had shone for a long time. Ryan didn't pay attention to them, but after reaching the bottom of the stairway, Ryan looked at the wall in habit, he had a clock on the wall in his apartment at the entrance. It was at this moment that he realized there were no clocks in the house.

It was peculiar that no one knew the time, yet they all gathered at a certain point with no notice. There was something out of the ordinary about this house. The walls held a secret that Ryan needed to figure out. Something wasn't right.

Ryan eventually made his way to the sliding door past the library. The library was empty except for a few burning coals in the fireplace. Ryan quickly made his way past it and out the sliding door.

There was a strong wind that blew sea mist into Ryan's eyes. They stung and teared, forcing Ryan to cover his face until the wind subsided. He stared out over the sea and saw that the morning sky was red. It was eerily beautiful. Ryan knew, however, that a red sky in the morning was not a good sign. Usually, there was a storm on its way.

Ryan walked out from the door onto the beach. Ryan took his shoes off and dug his toes into the sand, but the sand was cold and sent shivers up Ryan's spine. He shuddered but continued on his way. While walking, Ryan saw a dark rolling cloud heading toward him over the sea. There were a few stray bolts of lightning cracking through the cloud. Ryan felt uneasy and picked up his pace. Ryan rushed his way to the kitchen porch.

He kneeled and looked through the door into the kitchen. Ryan could barely make out a dark figure. The sea mist covered the door in a fine film and blurred the person. Either way, whoever it was could not see Ryan out here. Ryan crouched and snuck underneath the porch to where he first saw the hand, but Ryan couldn't find anything out of the ordinary. The sand was whipped up into small dunes, and there were no footprints or any strange objects out of place. Ryan sighed at his defeat.

I guess it was just all in my mind. What is happening to me?

His thought was interrupted by the sliding door. Ryan crouched even lower and held his breath as the wood creaked above him. Someone was walking out. The swollen wood groaned under their feet. Every squeak and pop made Ryan twitch. He waited until the footsteps stopped at the edge of the porch. He heard a large sigh and the person began talking to themselves.

Ryan couldn't make out much of the words. He began to shuffle his way toward whoever it was to be able to listen better, but the voice was still muffled. Ryan could make out some words, "plan…decision…solutions." It didn't make any sense to Ryan, but then he heard another voice speak and it was stunningly familiar. The voice stuttered, just like Frank did.

Ryan's adrenaline was pumping. His hands and feet went cold as he tried to stay as still as possible. Once the conversation was over, the floorboards creaked and groaned again as the person retreated to the house. Ryan waited to see if the second person would follow, but he never did. Ryan ducked out from under the stairs and slowly tried to stand up to see who was there but, but to his surprise, there was no one on the porch. Ryan was puzzled. He didn't hear the other person leave. Could it be possible they had left together while only making noise for one person? Ryan didn't think it possible and walked up the stairs toward the house in defeat. From the other side of the house, Cornelius stepped out from around the corner. He crossed his arms and watched Ryan retreat into the house with a disapproving scowl.

CHAPTER 23

Ryan entered the house, but something felt different. It did not provide friendly, peaceful air it previously did. Instead, the atmosphere was felt tense, almost like someone was watching him.

Ryan brushed off the feeling as best he could, but it lingered in his mind. Ryan was walking toward his room when he heard a noise coming from Frank's. The noise was subtly familiar: a faint huff of breath followed by a break and a sniffle. Ryan knocked lightly on the heavy door.

"Frank? You okay in there?" asked Ryan as softly as he could.

"I-I-I'm fine," sniffled Frank. "Don't worry."

Ryan wasn't convinced but he didn't want to press him further. He sighed and continued on his way to his room.

Once Ryan opened the door, there was a note on the floor of his room. Ryan shut the door and picked up the note. It was freshly torn, across the bottom corner. It looked like a page from the books in the library.

It had to be done. He can't stop what I'm beginning. There's no going back now. I had someone help me with it, so I think it's safe to say I have an accomplice. If he says anything I—

The rest of the page was ripped.

Ryan's heart began beating faster. He didn't know what to do. He stuffed the note into his pocket and rushed out his door. He ran down the hallway to Frank's door and knocked much more quickly now. There was no answer.

"Frank? Frank!" Ryan began pounding on the door now.

"What's going on?" asked a voice behind Ryan. He ignored him and continued to pound on the door.

Ryan felt the person grab his arm and stop him. He spun around and saw Cornelius with an angry scowl on his face.

"What are you doing?" asked Cornelius sternly.

The silence between them was thick and tense. It took a minute before Ryan responded.

"I think Frank is in trouble," responded Ryan, staring back at Cornelius.

Cornelius's expression turned from anger to curiosity. "How can you be so sure?" asked Cornelius quizzingly.

"Just open the door!" yelled Ryan. His nose began bleeding again.

Oh, not now. This is the last thing I need.
He wiped the blood from his nose and Cornelius was shocked. He fumbled his key out of his jacket pocket. He unlocked the door as quick as he could and both he and Ryan rushed into the room.

The only thing Ryan and Cornelius found was a trail of blood drops leading to the bathroom, the door was slightly ajar with the light on. Cornelius pushed the door open and fell to the ground on his knees. Ryan rushed in behind and gasped. He could feel the breath being knocked out of him. Frank was in the tub, the bright porcelain stained pink. His right arm was extended out past the rim and the blood was dripping over the edge. The stream of blood fell from the tub into the cracks of the tiles, reaching out like long bloody fingers.

On Frank's chest was carved, "It was me," in jagged letters. The blood was slowly streaming out of the letters.

Cornelius began crying and reached his hand up to Frank's neck. He waited for a second to confirm the inevitable, and covered his face and sobbed violently. Ryan sat down on the toilet seat, turning away from the violent scene. Tears fell from his eyes. While he and Frank weren't very close, he was Ryan's closest friend.

Ryan felt lost and confused. It was miserable. No one to talk to, no one to keep him company. Ryan's heart ached, but it was a familiar pain, something that never fully went away or healed. Ryan started to feel emotionally' numb. The constant trauma and battle he had with his heart was exhausting.

Ryan felt strange being at a funeral for a man he barely knew, and that was the truth of it: Frank was still a stranger to him. Ryan had also never been to a funeral in a backyard before, but Frank had stated he wanted a burial at sea. Ryan watched out along the ocean as Cornelius spoke a few words. It was incoherent to Ryan. Everything was a blur. The ocean waves crashing in the background, the breeze hitting his face, his itchy shirt scratching him under his blazer.

Ryan stared as Frank's departure made its way toward the ocean. He felt a tear roll down his cheek. Ryan inhaled the salty air and wiped the tear away. Ryan said his goodbyes and watched the skies. It was dark, and the storm was moving ever closer. Sharp lightning shot across the sky, ripping apart the clouds.

"Better we head inside," said Cornelius

Ryan looked over his shoulder and nodded slightly. He turned to face the impending storm once more before he turned to head inside the house.

Ryan felt different. Something about him changed. He felt numb and cold all the time. But there was something else, something stirring within him. He needed to find out why this happened.

Ryan knocked the sand off his shoes and entered the house. Without saying a word, he went up to his room and changed into more casual clothing. Ryan felt something he hadn't felt in a long time. Determination. Now he felt more determined to hunt the truth down, Ryan headed out of his room and locked it before he made his way to the library. In the kitchen, Ryan found Cornelius.

"How are you holding up, Ryan?" asked Cornelius.

"I'll be alright," Ryan responded as he grabbed a pear to snack on. "How about you?" Ryan asked back.

"I'll be okay, I think," Cornelius sniffled.

While Cornelius sounded sincere, he didn't look sad. Ryan was suspicious and was going to pursue it, but he didn't have time for it. Instead, he felt it would be better to gather some evidence from the books in the library. He walked out of the room and entered the library, the sun was shining brightly through the room and Ryan turned to the bookshelves that lined the walls. There were hundreds, maybe thousands of books, and one of them might have a ripped page that could help Ryan.

Ryan grabbed a handful of books at a time. He searched and flipped through all the pages. They seemed distantly familiar, stories that he already knew or some that related to his own life. Ryan searched entire bookshelves as the time ticked by. The moon was shining brightly before

Ryan finished his search. He couldn't find anything. Ryan was confused but he didn't give up hope. He continued to look through the entire room: under the couch, in between the cushions, but couldn't find the matching ripped page Ryan slumped in the recliner and rubbed the temples of his head with his hand. While trying to figure out the source of the paper, Ryan dozed off.

When Ryan finally opened his eyes, he found himself at the entrance of a cemetery. The fog was very dense, the trees were barren of all leaves, and a crisp fall breeze surrounded him. The air wafted through Ryan's nose, but it's cold temperature didn't sting.

Ryan looked around. There was no sign for the name of the cemetery. Ryan grabbed the black, cold metal fence posts. He didn't feel frightened or alarmed. In fact, he felt at peace. Ryan saw a small opening in the fog with a small tombstone in the middle. Ryan looked at it curiously and decided to walk toward it. The fog thickened as he walked, and the air became harder to breathe. Ryan felt his lungs ache for oxygen, but he pushed onward.

The fog thickened to a point where everything around Ryan was a hazy white. No shadows, no colors. Just haze. Ryan felt his strength falter as he quivered for air. He opened his mouth, but nothing would enter.

Eventually, Ryan broke through the fog and came to the clearing. He dropped to his knees and took a large breath. The air burned inside him, but he continued to take deep breaths of the desperately needed air. Once his breathing was under control, Ryan cleared his throat and stood up slowly, one leg at a time. Ryan blinked several times. His hard breathing had brought tears to his eyes. With his vision cleared, Ryan began walking again toward the tombstone. Ryan crouched and tried to read the name, but it was illegible. He could faintly make out the first letter as "L."

Ryan sighed and stood up again. He turned away from the tombstone and found himself staring at the fog. Out of the fog came forward an image: a visage of Hannah— the lifeless version that he found in the hospital. But this Hannah was different. This Hannah looked like a body made of fog, like Ryan was looking through frosted glass. It wasn't fully whole, just a distorted memory of an image.

"Is this your grave?" asked Ryan.

You're not afraid anymore, whispered the voice. Its mouth never moved but Ryan heard the words dance around his ears. It was faint but still there. Like the ghostly image, the words rang but faded quickly. Ryan shook his head in response.

This is my grave, after I died, responded the voice.

"were you a tenant of Cornelius?" muttered Ryan.

I do not know who I am, just one memory lingers. said the hushed voice.

"What would that be" Asked Ryan

Cornelius is hiding many things, if you are not careful, this could be your grave as well. Or maybe it is too late, whispered the voice.

"I know. What can I do to figure it out?" quizzed Ryan.

The image began to fade and turned its back on Ryan as it retreated toward the fog. He turned back toward the grave and, on a whim, Ryan asked one more question.

"Do you know where I can find the book that I'm looking for?"

No.

Ryan nodded and continued watching the grave.

It may be in your best interest to search Cornelius' room.

Ryan looked back at the figure but it was gone. He felt the ground tremble and felt himself fade away from the dream.

When Ryan woke he realized it was clearly after midnight. Ryan stood up from his chair and decided to head back toward his room. There was a light emitting from Cornelius' room which was slightly ajar. Ryan pushed on the door slightly and it groaned loudly. Inside, Ryan saw the room was empty.

The room was neatly kept. The bed sheets were tightly made, there was a small lamp turned on sitting on the nightstand, and underneath the lamp was a picture of a couple, which Ryan promptly ignored. He was more interested in the gold key that shone in front of it. Ryan placed his fingers on the key. It was weirdly warm, but there was a creaking upon the stairs and Ryan panicked, leaving the room hastily without taking the key.

Ryan rushed back to the front of his door and slid the key into the lock. Ryan heard Cornelius's voice call out to him.

"Are you just getting back?" he asked.

"Yeah, I fell asleep in the library. Just worn out from the grief," said Ryan.

Cornelius looked at Ryan suspiciously but did not continue the conversation.

Ryan looked over at Cornelius once more and said with a smirk, "Well, goodnight," and shut the door behind him.

Cornelius grunted and replied solemnly, "Night."

Closing the door, Ryan moved quickly. He remembered he had taken a book from earlier in his trip when he had arrived. He searched all over his room and eventually found it snuggly under his bed. Ryan opened the book and fumbled through the pages, looking for any torn piece of paper anywhere. Alas, there was nothing.

Ryan tossed the book onto the bed beside him. He looked up in the air and sighed. He shut his eyes for a moment. The searching was wearing him out. His eyes were strained and dry. Ryan kept them shut for a while before he toppled over fast asleep.

The next morning, Ryan stirred in his bed. His clothes were tight against him and his skin felt suffocated. Ryan stripped his clothes off to take a shower. He opened the door and immediately saw a flashback of Frank in the bathtub. Ryan's head hurt when he saw it and he shut his eyes. When he reopened them, the image was gone.

Ryan brushed off the encounter as his grief coming to haunt him, but this wasn't the first time he saw something that wasn't there. Nonetheless, Ryan turned the shower on and proceeded to take a very hot shower to try and clear his mind.

When Ryan was finished, it was time for breakfast. Ryan changed into some fresh clothes and headed out of his room, locking the door behind him. He made his way down to the dining room but, to his surprise, no one was there. Ryan walked into the kitchen but could find no one.

Looking out the French sliding doors, Ryan could see raindrops appear on the window. Dark clouds swirled around above the house, the storm was here.

Ryan pressed his hand on the glass. He shivered as the cold quickly traveled up his spine. His skin was covered in goose bumps, and it was only elevated by the voice that appeared from behind him.

"You're going to leave handprints," said the voice. It was slightly familiar and more feminine than Cornelius's.

Ryan turned around to face the voice and was surprised to see a familiar woman standing behind him. It was the same blonde that ignored him days earlier.

Ryan raised his eyebrow and motioned his hand toward her in a questioning way.

"Now you want to talk to me?" he said with a slight smile.

Amy's expression turned grim. "Cut the bullshit, okay? I'm here to warn you. Something is wrong in this place. People have been disappearing and no one knows why."

There was a creak in the floorboards above their heads, and Amy looked over her shoulder.

"We can't talk here," she said in a hushed voice.

She moved closer to Ryan, and he instinctively backed up, but she didn't notice. Her mouth was right up against his ear. He could feel the cold window pushing on his back now, the rain sending little vibrations through his body.

"Meet me in the library after dark. We'll talk then," she said in a whisper. She turned and left the room before Ryan could utter a word.

Ryan had to wait until dark, but that wouldn't be for a while. Ryan had no idea what he could do in the meantime but decided to go and find Cornelius for breakfast.

Ryan made his way up the stairs to Cornelius's door. He knocked three times and waited for an answer. When no answer came, he knocked three more times before he finally heard his voice.

"Who is it?" he yelled at the door.

"Hi, Cornelius. Good morning. It's Ryan," Ryan said, flustered. He was taken aback by the response, He wasn't sure Cornelius was really in there.

There was a moment of silence before Ryan could hear the door clicking to unlock and then swing open. On the other side, Cornelius stood without a blazer or tie, and his hair was clearly disheveled. He looked around Ryan into the corridor with the same paranoia that Amy had.

"Well? What do you want?" he said hastily.

"I was just wondering if we were going to have breakfast?" responded Ryan slowly.

"If you want breakfast, make it yourself. All the ingredients are there. People don't come down for breakfast anymore," Cornelius replied as he closed the door on Ryan.

Ryan continued standing at the door before he realized it was pointless. Ryan made his way back to the kitchen and had a bowl of cereal before heading back to his room.

The time moved slowly. It was maddening to Ryan. He tried to wait as patiently as a child before Christmas morning. A yearning to find the mysterious gift haunted him every minute as time slowly carried on.

Ryan paced around his room. He could not keep his mind focused, and he needed to distract himself from it. He decided at this point, it would be best to begin packing his things. As the situation was getting dire, it was probably best if Ryan left, even if he had to pay for his own medical bills. Ryan began grabbing all of his clothes and belongings and stuffing them into the suitcase he had. Leaving nothing to chance, he didn't bother to even fold them. As he pulled a shirt from the dresser drawer, there was a soft clunk of an object hitting the drawer's wooden bottom.

Ryan dropped the shirt, he peered into the drawer. Inside lay the leather-bound box that Hannah had given him.

Ryan drew in a shaky breath. He tried to control his emotions and slowly reached into the drawer. The box was softer than Ryan remembered it. It was delicate but sturdy at the same time. Ryan took a deep breath and ran his thumb to the corner and began to lift it. It creaked with anticipation, but there was a knock at the door.

Ryan was startled by the sound initially. He placed the box back inside he drawer and shut it. He opened the door to find Cornelius standing at the entrance, the same way as Ryan had moments earlier.

"What do you want for lunch?" he said, wiping sweat from his forehead with a handkerchief. He was much less formal in the way he spoke. Something was definitely wrong.

"I'm not sure yet, I only just ate breakfast," replied Ryan, holding the door with his hand.

Cornelius grunted and turned away. He began walking away when he said, "If you want anything, let me know or get it yourself," he said coldly.

Ryan nodded and shut the door. It was by far the strangest way he'd seen Cornelius.

CHAPTER 24

Finally, the sun set and it was soon time to meet Amy in the library. The storm was now in full swing, and the winds were devastating. It was so loud from the constant bombardment of rain and wind that there was never a silent moment in the house. Nevertheless, Ryan made his way through the corridors in the dark.

When he reached the kitchen, he fumbled around to find the candle and matches Cornelius had left them. Once Ryan found it, he quickly lit the candle and it surrounded the room in a warm glow. Ryan began to make his way to the library. Ryan did not have to be mindful of his footing as the storm drowned out the noise of the floorboards. Ryan could see a bright light from the library. He assumed Amy was already in there.

Upon entering the library, he noticed that the fireplace had a tremendous fire going, much larger than usual. The furniture had also been rearranged. There was a recliner in the middle of the room with its back to Ryan. He walked carefully toward it, looking over his shoulder a couple times.

"Amy? Amy is that you?" he said in a hushed voice.

There was no response.

"Amy?" Ryan said again in a slightly louder tone.

Ryan reached his hand out and grabbed ahold of the back of the recliner. He twisted the chair around. Ryan screamed at the sight and dropped his candle. The smell of smoke filled his nostrils.

Ryan retched and fell to the ground. Amy was sitting the chair, her throat cut and her eyes plucked out. The blood had dropped down her front and caked the whole recliner in it. Ryan couldn't breathe. His lungs were gasping for air, aching at every heartbeat. Ryan stared at the floor, Amy's face burned into his brain.

"She was frankly quite beautiful. It's a shame," boomed a voice above Ryan.

It hurt Ryan's stomach to turn his gaze from the floor. He stayed on his hands and knees, watching the floor with two polished dress shoes walking toward him. They stopped just at his eye level. Ryan struggled to lean back to see who it was, but he already knew.

Cornelius squatted beside Ryan. He looked at him directly, the firelight dancing across his eyes. Ryan stared but could say nothing. He was still trying to catch his breath. He felt cold sweat dripping down the side of his face.

Cornelius flashed a small dagger at Ryan. It was covered in blood. He tilted it toward Amy.

"You know why I had to do that, right?" he said with an evil smirk. He looked proud of what he had done to her.

"You monster," Ryan uttered. Saying the words made him retch again.

"Come now, Ryan. No need for name calling." Cornelius held his grin. "I told them specifically to obey my plans and my orders, but they didn't listen."

Cornelius stood slowly, his back toward Ryan.

"They disobeyed ME!" he shouted, each word coming out louder and louder. "They had what was coming to them!"

Cornelius turned his head back toward Ryan, grinning once again. --"But now, it's all over," he said calmly.

"What are you talking about? What's wrong with you?" screamed Ryan. He felt disgusted. His feeling of nausea never left, but he had managed to keep his breakfast down with what little strength he had.

Cornelius roared with laughter

"You just don't get it, do you? I thought you were smarter than this, Ryan," said Cornelius. He turned away from Ryan, stretched his arms wide, and let them fall to his sides.

Thunder cracked outside and shook the house. Ryan could feel the vibrations in his hands and knees.

"This was all for you. I did this for you," Cornelius mumbled. "It wasn't supposed to end like this, but what choice do I have," he said to himself. He clenched the dagger tighter.

"What do you mean?" persisted Ryan. "Tell me what's going on."

Cornelius gazed over his shoulder at Ryan, and chuckled as he did. He turned and began walking toward him slowly.

"You know, Ryan, we had a good run. I suppose it's only fair to tell you," Cornelius said. "I'm surprised you didn't figure it out sooner," He began.

"I know you're the murderer. Amy and I were coming to confront you," Ryan spoke as he tried to stand up.

Cornelius once again laughed.

"How wrong you are," Cornelius said smugly, with that sly grin. "I told Amy to tell you that to lure you here because I thought I could save you, but there's no saving you now. Everything is ruined."

"You keep saying that, explain yourself!" yelled Ryan.

"I warned them, but they didn't listen," said Cornelius ignoring Ryan`s demand.

"You warned them of what?" asked Ryan quietly.

"Of you," Cornelius said flatly, now looking in the distance.

"Are we just going to keep dancing around this? What about me?" asked Ryan

"You are the start and end to it all Ryan, when you arrived that's when they were supposed to listen to me without question," said Cornelius quietly

"No question? You can't control these people, they came here with the hope you would help them!" yelled Ryan back.

"People? There are no real people here, dear boy, including yourself," Cornelius said with a chuckle.

Ryan stared at Cornelius, puzzled, his mouth slightly open.

"You see Ryan, these 'people' as you call them are not actually here," he said, pointing the dagger to the recliner. "Go ahead, take a look."

Ryan spun around and looked at the now empty reclining chair. Its polished leather showed the firelight's gleam.

Ryan stared at the chair, flabbergasted. It was empty like nothing had happened.

"See?" said Cornelius, grinning. "There's nothing to worry about." He tilted his head in a profound manner.

"Th-that's not-t possible," Ryan stumbled to get the words out.

"In a normal world, no. But this isn't a normal world, Ryan," replied Cornelius.

"What are you even saying? Do you hear yourself? You're making no sense!" screamed Ryan.

"Maybe not yet, but everything will be unveiled in time," said Cornelius, opening his arms wide again.

Thunder boomed once more in the distance. It shook the house again, but much more violently this time. The chandelier jangled above them, clinking with every sway, the firelight glinting off it.

"The storm is getting closer, Ryan. Soon enough, this house may not stand any longer," said Cornelius hesitantly, creeping toward Ryan.

"Wait! Can you please tell me what's going on? I beg of you," Ryan said, tears in his eyes.

"I may as well tell you what's happening, I don't see any of us surviving this," Cornelius breathed, continuously walking toward Ryan. "So, I will ease you into it as best as I can."

He stopped in front of him for a second but then continued to walk. He made his way to the recliner and sat down, resting the dagger on the arm of the chair. He brushed his now unkempt hair out of his face.

"You're dying," Cornelius said calmly.
Ryan twitched his head to the side and breathed a small breath

"I said tell me the truth," Ryan said sternly.

"I am," he responded with that same condescending head tilt. "On the night of the accident, Hannah did not actually turn the car toward her side. In fact, she turned it the other way and let you have all the damage."

Cornelius paused, taking in a breath

"Now, I can't say it was intentional, but I do believe it was. Either way, the accident left you in critical condition, your body was broken. The excessive amount of damage to repair you took all of your mind's focus. That's why we're here. This was supposed to be the haven to ease you back into your body. To slowly have you take over control again." Cornelius explained.

"You're lying," Ryan said. His arms shook as he pushed himself up. The tears streamed down his face now.

"I'm not," Cornelius hissed. "You asked for the truth and I'm giving it to you. Listen to the whole thing and then make your assessment.

"Now then, when you were brought to the hospital, you had some severe nightmares. The nightmares were, in fact, your body willing your mind to reconnect but it was much too early, that's why they were frightening and unsettling," Cornelius said, pausing to take another breath.

"Unfortunately, you didn't face the nightmares head on. You ran from them, thus running further from your body, in essence. Now, as a last ditch effort to save us I disguised myself as Dr. Ulric to get a better understanding of you and how badly you were broken—sorry—fractured." Cornelius waved his hand in the air. "I knew you needed something to tick you off to come join me. I sent the bills and the outstanding payments and collection letters. It was all me."

"Wait, so you're saying this is all fake? Like a movie set?" Ryan asked, puzzled. He was pacing the room now.

"In a sense. I created everything based on our memories, we've always wanted a house by the beach so here we are. This is all happening right now inside your mind," Cornelius said, pointing a finger at Ryan.

"You're absolutely mental. You know that?" Ryan responded.

"Again, just wait for the end," Cornelius said stubbornly.

"So, I needed to lure you here with something that you wanted. I arranged it all so you could be eased into this idea and slowly regain control of your body to save us all. it worked for some time," Cornelius said flatteringly.

"But then things took a turn. My plan was to ease you into this and slowly piece you back together like a scattered puzzle, but some things got in the way," Cornelius said quietly.

"What things?" said Ryan, now interested in this cunning story.

"Your emotions mainly," Cornelius said with a sigh. He was now spinning the dagger that lay on the arm of the recliner.

"You see, your anger manifested itself violently and began to cause trouble. I had to take care of that trouble to protect you. I couldn't shock your mind into knowing what was happening," said Cornelius.

"What do you mean manifested itself?" asked Ryan.

"Well, you are in a traumatic state. It's only natural, but I didn't believe it to be such a problem," Cornelius responded.

"The 'tenants' that reside here are not actually people, as I have mentioned," Cornelius said, now looking at the floor.

"The tenants were my emotions?" Ryan said softly. He felt dizzy and fell backward into another recliner. It had just appeared out of thin air. Ryan looked at Cornelius who had his hand up in the air at Ryan.

"Anyway," Cornelius said, waving his hand, "the point is I would have saved you, Ryan. You continue to live, but I'm not sure for how much longer."

"Of course I'm alive. I'm right here!" yelled Ryan. He felt frustrated. This wasn't possible. It made no sense.

"You are the manifestation of yourself. It's a transition. I had to create something that you could latch onto," Cornelius said softly.

"Wait," said Ryan sternly. "If I'm me, the tenants are my emotions…. What does that make you?" asked Ryan, pointing a finger at Cornelius.

"I am a form of your conscious," responded Cornelius. See, in a normal mind, you would have one consciousness and you wouldn't know any different. I was the little voice inside your head, the thoughts you have, the one that keeps you present. But after the accident, your corpus callosum was severed causing my creation."

"So you're saying we`re two parts of my mind? Together?" asked Ryan, even more confused than before.

"In a sense, yes. I believe you're in a hospital somewhere. I no longer have control of your body, so I'm not sure what happened. All I know is that you are alive, otherwise we would not be here," said Cornelius grimly.

Thunder struck again, more violently than ever this time. Dust fell from the ceiling onto Ryan's shoulders. He brushed it off.

"So this house is what exactly?" asked Ryan bleakly

"Think of it as our housing unit, its where we normally are in ideal conditions," Cornelius said looking towards the fire.

"Time is running out, Ryan. This house will not stand much longer against the storm. What's your decision?" Cornelius said, trying to yell over the thunder.

"My decision?" Ryan looked down at his hands. It all felt too real to be made up. What was his game? Ryan's head throbbed.

Suddenly, an awareness came to Ryan.

"Before I do, I need to get something," Ryan said, standing up.

"You'd better hurry," Cornelius said, also standing.

Ryan left the library and ran up toward his room, skipping two stairs at a time. He frantically unlocked his door and went straight for the dresser. He opened the dresser drawer and pulled out the small black box inside.

Ryan took the box and left the room, leaving it unlocked. He returned to the library where Cornelius was standing facing the flames.

"This will tell me the truth," he said, flashing the box at Cornelius.

"Oh, this should be good," Cornelius' gaze never left the fire.

Ryan scoffed and sat back down in the recliner. He set the box on his lap in front of him and took a deep breath. He began to open the box slowly. Cornelius's head arched upward but still faced the fire. Ryan watched as the box creaked open.

Inside on a black chain was a perfectly intact, sunset colored, heart shaped jewel.

Ryan felt the air leave his chest. His hands began shaking and he dropped the box onto the floor, the fire burning as a reflection in the jewel. Cornelius laughed quietly to himself.

"Do you believe me now?" Cornelius said, still fixating himself on the fire. "I told you, but you chose not to listen."

CHAPTER 25

Cornelius stood and walked towards the fireplace, he raised his open hand towards the spines of the books, he ran his finger down the spines horizontally.

"We had a good life," sighed Cornelius.

Cornelius held the dagger in one hand and flicked the tip with his other.

"Well, my boy, I believe it's time," Cornelius said, but as he began to turn around, a gold chain wrapped around his neck.

Cornelius grabbed at the chain, trying to pull himself free as the chain wound itself tightly around his throat, gripping tightly. The air in his lungs burned, his eyes felt as though they were going to pop out of his head, blood rushed to his face, and he began sweating. Cornelius pulled at the chain with his free hand and thrust the knife behind him. The blade moved through the air unobstructed.

Cornelius bent down toward the flames and tried to wriggle himself free but to no avail. Just as the darkness began creeping over him, with one last thrust of energy Cornelius felt the knife stick. He felt warm liquid flow over his hand but his hearing began cutting out. He felt his heartbeat slow and his eyes grew fuzzy. He uttered what he could but nothing was tangible.

Cornelius reached into his pocket and pulled out a small picture. It was of him and a woman holding hands and laughing. He stared at the picture until his eyes rolled up and he fell to the floor.

CHAPTER 26

Ryan crouched over Cornelius's body, panting. He unwound the chain from his neck and picked up the fallen picture it was of himself and Hannah at the beach a few years back. As he flipped it over, there was writing on the back: *Beach day with Hannah, 2008.*

Ryan remembered that day fondly, it was one of the last few dates they had as a couple. Was it possible that Cornelius wasn't lying after all?

Ryan held the chain in his hand and the jewel swung like a metronome. He raised it to his eye level and watched as the firelight danced inside it. It enhanced the jewel's color and it shimmered brightly. Ryan placed the necklace around his neck and walked toward the bookshelves, clutching his abdomen. He was bleeding profusely. He picked several copies of the books and took them to the recliner. He sat the stack on the floor and picked up the very top one. He opened it to the very first page and began reading.

They were all of his memories. Ryan could only assume that Cornelius had been responsible for it. He changed the language to make it seem like an independent story, but they were now very clear to Ryan. Ryan laughed at one particular memory he read. It was one of Hannah and himself, Ryan had made Hannah laugh so hard the drink came out of her nose, Ryan remembered laughing so hard his sides and his cheeks ached with joy.

Ryan continued to read through the book as the house around him began collapsing. The ceiling opened up with huge chunks falling down around Ryan. Ryan absorbed the memories and continued to read as his world fell apart. His memories filled him up with joy, looking at the past and seeing his great experiences. It was a relief to finally be released from the prison of his own creation.

CHAPTER 27

Outside of the hospital room, Hannah stood idly by, sniffling and rubbing her red and swollen eyes. She had cried so much it'd begun to hurt. A nurse came out of the room.

"Okay, you can go back in," she said with a quickly fading smile.

Hannah sniffled once more and nodded slowly. She headed back into the room. Each time she did it made her heart sink a little lower. Ryan was hooked up to several machines, several of which were beeping and making noise. Hannah sat down next to him, watching his chest being pumped full of air, then deflating once more. He had lost so much weight, his ribs were clearly visible. She had stray tears drop down her cheek every few minutes, she couldn't control it anymore.

The pain was too much. It hurt every day, and the nonstop crying drained her to sleep every night. She grabbed Ryan's lifeless hand as she did every night and held on tight.

"I'm sorry I did this to you. I wish I had convinced you to stay that day. I just want you to get better," cried Hannah softly. "I love you, Ryan. I hope you know that."

She clenched his hand tight and brought it to her lips. She kissed his hand gently. He smelled like medicine.

As she was lowering his hand, she could feel him grip tighter. Hannah looked in disbelief. She could have sworn she felt it. But in a second, it was gone. And so was he.

The machines started raining alarms and the drone of the absent heartbeat lingered in Hannah's ears. Everything faded, the noise and the chatter.

Time is a cruel friend, always around when you don't want it, and yet always out of reach when you run out of it. Ryan's time was up and there was nothing Hannah could do to keep him here. The sand in his hourglass had finally fallen to the bottom, and she was left to count the rest of her days without him.

Hannah's heart shattered. She felt so fragile and so vulnerable, raw and hurting.

The days that followed seemed like a blur, a wave of people and questions and preparations until the day arrived. Hannah approached Ryan's dark casket and placed a single red rose on top. Around the rose hung the chain of the now broken necklace. There was one large shard attached to the chain still. Hannah felt the tears come as the casket was lowered into the ground.

As Hannah returned to her apartment, something felt different. She removed her jacket and placed her keys where her kitchen table once was, but they clanged as they hit the floor. She sighed and dabbed her eyes. She knelt to pick up her keys when she noticed in the place of the keys was a golden envelope.

Her name was written on the front with beautiful metallic red script handwriting. On the other side laid a large red wax seal with the letter "C" on it.

About the Author

Ottavio Lepore was born in Mola di Bari, Italy and currently lives in New York, USA. From his youth, he had a passion for writing and wrote several short stories and poems all throughout his academic career with *The Fractured Mind* being his first official published work.

Made in the USA
Middletown, DE
23 January 2019